"I don't want you to leave."

Brad stopped Amanda's departure with both words and action. He reached for her, putting his arms around her.

But when he would have pulled her close, her fist balled on his chest, preventing him. Their eyes locked, heat darting between them. "Brad, I need to go."

Several seconds passed. The air crackled with passion, with attraction. His gaze settled on her full lips and he burned to taste her. "Don't go." He waited for a sign to take what he wanted.

Slowly she melted into him. He reveled in the feel of her soft curves against his body, her breasts pressing into his chest. Her fists opened, fingers spreading and moving to his shoulders to tug him closer.

Finally they were kissing. Wildly, passionately. Tongues mating, stroke for stroke. He wanted this woman. And nothing would stop him from having her...now.

Dear Reader,

Writing for Harlequin Blaze is exciting, because I have always enjoyed the way these stories embrace the excitement and sensuality of new love. The heat of those first kisses. A shiver from a mere brush of the hand. There is nothing like it, is there?

Writing *Hard and Fast* was fun because professional baseball players can appear bigger than life in so many ways, yet they have these superstitions that make them very real. My son has a friend whose father is a professional baseball player. I had the opportunity to interview someone who could offer insight into this world. The interview rolled along nicely until I asked about locker-room talk. He was quite concerned about offending my virgin ears! Once I assured him I wouldn't be offended, we had a blast chatting about the down and dirty behind-the-scenes action—the fun stuff!

I hope you enjoy the players in the locker room as much as I did. And even more so, I hope you fall in love with Brad and Amanda.

Lisa Renee Jones

HARD
AND FAST
Lisa Renee Jones

TORONTO • NEW YORK • LONDON
AMSTERDAM • PARIS • SYDNEY • HAMBURG
STOCKHOLM • ATHENS • TOKYO • MILAN • MADRID
PRAGUE • WARSAW • BUDAPEST • AUCKLAND

ISBN-13: 978-0-373-79343-3
ISBN-10:   0-373-79343-X

HARD AND FAST

This edition published by arrangement with Harlequin Books S.A.

® and TM are trademarks of the publisher. Trademarks indicated with
® are registered in the United States Patent and Trademark Office, the
Canadian Trade Marks Office and in other countries.

www.eHarlequin.com

Printed in U.S.A.

ABOUT THE AUTHOR

Lisa lives in Austin, Texas, where she spends her days writing the dreams playing in her head. Before becoming a writer, Lisa lived the life of a corporate executive, often taking the red-eye flight out of town and flying home for the excitement of a Little League baseball game. Visit Lisa at Lisareneejones.com.

My thanks to:

Razor Shines for the interview
Matt & Ronald for the baseball insight!
Diego for believing when I didn't
My mom for supporting my dream

1

AMANDA WRIGHT was living a dream.

New shoes. Expensive outfit—also new. Press pass around her neck allowing entry into a professional baseball players' locker room—a room certain to display hot male bodies in various stages of undress.

It was the perfect female fantasy come to life.

Or it should have been.

But right now, Amanda felt as if she were about to walk into the lions' den and those lions—aka ballplayers—were going to eat her alive.

Her high heels clicked on the concrete floor of the tunnel leading to the Los Angeles Rays' locker room, her toes pinched and her mind raced. Her journalistic instincts buzzed with the thought of the after-game activity on the other side of the door. Still, she hung back, wishing like hell she could tap her heels together and transport herself back to Dallas, Texas.

Dallas, the place where she'd had a position reporting high school sports for one of the daily newspapers. It didn't matter that her work had lacked any semblance of challenge and leaned dangerously close to boring. She'd had job security. And her parents and her sister. She'd had her comfortable little downtown apartment overlooking White Rock Lake—she really loved that view.

Nerves flooded her system, and she stopped. For a moment, Amanda stood, watching people pass. What would she do if she went into that locker room and made a fool of herself? What would happen if she didn't impress her editor with her first column? Or didn't attract readers?

What had she been thinking? She must have been insane to leave her comfortable life behind. And for what? A sports column with her name attached? Didn't seem like such a sweet deal at this moment.

She took a deep breath. A *dream* column, she reminded herself. On game days she got space in the paper no matter what, just as she had back home. But now she'd hit the big time. Twice a week she had her very own feature in the sports section. And this wasn't high school baseball. This was the majors. An opportunity she'd fantasized about for years.

But, of course, the job had come with extreme pressure. There was one tiny condition she hadn't shared with her family because they'd only worry more than they already were. Her new boss, Kevin Jones, had given her a short time frame in which to build a readership or she'd be gone. Seemed her predecessor had left and taken many of his fans with him. When she'd asked Kevin how short, he'd simply said, "Short."

The ringing of her cell phone offered a welcomed excuse to continue to stall. She shoved a wayward strand of long, auburn hair behind her ear and reached inside her purse, a petite Louis Vuitton bag her sister, Kelli, had given her to celebrate the new job.

The minute Amanda hit the Answer button, her sister's voice snapped through the line, a lightning rod of reprimand. "I knew it."

"Knew what?"

Kelli ignored the question. "Why are you answering your phone?"

Amanda rolled her eyes. "Why are you calling if you don't want me to answer?"

"Because I knew you would," Kelli retorted. "I didn't want to be right, but I knew I would be. Shouldn't you be in a locker room full of hot bodies, drooling enough for the both of us?"

"How do you know I'm not?"

"Like you'd answer if you were." A pause followed and in her mind's eye, Amanda could see Kelli shaking her head. "You've worked yourself into a state of self-doubt, haven't you? Why do you always do this to yourself?"

"I'm not doing anything," Amanda said, lying. Kelli was right. Amanda tended to let big events work her into a ball of nerves, so much so that she often would get sick. Every year, the first day of school had been greeted with a horrible cold and a red nose. Before a swim meet, she'd have abdominal cramps from the knots in her stomach. It was a miracle she'd managed to perform so well, time after time.

"Right," Kelli said. "I wasn't born yesterday. You're standing on the wrong side of that door talking yourself out of this dream."

"Okay, so I am or I was or—"

"Stop trying to think of excuses. You've wanted your own column for years. It's the only thing you've talked about with excitement since you left competitive swimming. You can do this. You've been doing it for years."

Amanda hadn't *left* swimming. Her knee injury had stolen her aspirations. Shoving away the thought, she reminded herself that period in her life was history and should be buried. The here and now counted and she had new mountains to climb. Or, rather, locker rooms to conquer.

"I covered high school events," she reminded her optimistic sister, stepping out of the path of passersby and leaning against the wall. "These are professional ballplayers."

"You've dealt with plenty of professional athletes."

Following her NFL team doctor dad while she was a teen did not count. "Years ago!"

"Well then, you better come home," Kelli said. "Absolutely, you are in over your head. You could get your old job back. You know you could."

Amanda absorbed the sarcastic comments as a much-needed reality check. She'd spent years trying to get away from the high school grind. Her ex-husband had been rooted in Dallas and had refused to move, determined to work himself into her father's good graces and the better opportunities—a higher-end clientele along with the status and money that accompanied it—to which he had access. Her ex had cared about those things more than her. After being sideswiped by his affairs, she'd welcomed the divorce, but had needed the security of having family nearby.

Now, she'd found the courage to land her dream job, to relocate, and she couldn't blow it. Not now. She had to do this. She pushed off the wall and straightened.

"I don't know if I should curse you for your snarky attitude or thank you," Amanda said.

"You're welcome. Now go get 'em, girl. With all that sass and your hot new image, you're gonna kick butt. Which outfit are you wearing?"

Amanda smiled, thinking of shopping with her sister a month before. That had been the day Amanda had decided to make herself over with a new, sexier appearance and take on the world with a new attitude.

"The black Jones New York skirt," she informed Kelli. She loved her new look. Why she'd hidden in long skirts and flat sandals for so long, she didn't know.

Actually, she did know. She'd been so completely absorbed in competitive swimming that nothing else had seemed important. When her knee injury had burst that dream, her ex-husband's career had easily taken center stage. It had been as if she'd lost herself, her very identity stripped. She'd been Amanda the swimmer who'd become Amanda the wife. Nowhere in there was space for Amanda the woman or Amanda the reporter.

Her makeover changed more than her outside. It gave her confidence and transitioned her into a new state of mind that was dedicated to finding herself and her dreams again. That change of perspective had helped her shine in her job interview.

"Very nice," Kelli said, approval in her tone. "The skirt is one of my favorite picks. Did you go with the Bandolino sandals with those cute ankle straps?"

"Ah, yeah, though I regret letting you talk me into them. They're killing my feet."

"Smile through it, sis. They look sexy and that's what counts. Now kisses and kick butt." The line went dead.

Amanda smiled and slid her phone into her purse. She hitched the strap over her shoulder, prepared to take charge of the locker room and, if she got lucky, a few good men along the way.

With that in mind, she charged forward, no longer caring about the pinch of her toes. No longer letting nerves get in her way. She had a hot new image and a hot new job. No way was she going to stop moving forward now.

In fact, she decided arriving a little late might be good. The guys wouldn't be expecting her. Their guards would be down and she'd get her story.

But it wasn't their guards that fell as she entered that locker room. It was hers.

Surrounded by half-naked, gorgeous men, Amanda's eyes went wide. Everywhere she looked she found rippling muscle and rock-hard backsides exposed by gaping towels. For a girl who hadn't had sex in so long it was embarrassing, the sight was downright shocking. Okay, arousing.

She should have been prepared for this. After all, she'd been in plenty of locker rooms with her father. Clearly, years of working the high school circuit had made her forget just how delicious grown men could be.

And these grown men—correction, half-naked, hot grown men—were *all* staring at her as the noise had dissolved into silence.

Suddenly, Amanda's bravado of moments before slipped into hiding. Her slim-cut skirt—the one that seemed so perfect only moments before—now felt revealing.

"Hi," she said, waving nervously, while promising herself she would *not* look below the waist to the display of muscled thighs and teeny-weensy towels. "I'm the new reporter for the *Tribune*." She reached for the badge hanging from a chain around her neck and held it up.

She was met with a few smiles and murmured hellos. Some turned away, curiosity satisfied. Many continued to stare. Without conscious effort, she did exactly what she'd vowed not to do. Her gaze dropped and took in several sets of rather enticing male torsos, complete with defined abdominals. Worse, before she realized what she was doing, she swiped a strand of hair off her forehead, trying to get a better view.

Afraid she would be caught peeking, Amanda snapped her attention to eye level. She'd come here for a story, and not just any story—one for her very own sports column. Her reaction proved, however, that she needed to address her state of sexual deprivation. Otherwise, being in the company of these men would pose a real distraction.

"Great game, guys," Amanda said, smiling. "Who wants to be the headliner for my first story?"

"You've got to be kidding." The voice came from Amanda's left. A thirty-something man, wearing a sports coat and jeans, stepped into view. His piercing black eyes gave her a rude sweep from head to toe. "Has Kevin lost his mind?"

"Kevin?" Amanda asked, her eyebrows dipping, thinking. She'd come into town only the day before and met the staff at the paper in a whirlwind that morning. But there was only one Kevin she remembered. "As in my boss, Kevin?"

He crossed his arms in front of his plaid-covered chest before she could locate a press badge. "I'm surprised he didn't go for blond and big-breasted."

Who was this jerk? Amanda didn't know nor did she care. Everything that happened here and now set a tone for the future. She wasn't about to be made a fool of her first day on the job.

Amanda gave the jerk a bored look. "And who might you be?"

"Jack Krass," he said, a slight gloat to his tone that said she should know the name.

And she did, as did the rest of the city. Jack Krass's face was plastered on billboards—lots of them—advertising his column with a competing paper. She should have recognized him. Amanda had replaced him at the *Tribune,* meaning he'd once worn the shoes she now had to prove she could walk in. Worse, they were shoes two other reporters before her had failed to fill. Even though his confidence could be justified, in Amanda's mind there was no call for him to be snide and nasty.

"Your name sounds vaguely familiar," she said, a finger to her chin in mock concentration. "Wait!" She pointed in the air. "I know how I know you. A bunch of the guys at the paper were playing pin the tail on the Jack Krass this morning." Her eyes went wide. "Wow. That must mean they really don't like you. Why is that?"

A roar of laughter drew Amanda's attention to the handsome face of Brad Rogers, who shared her hometown in Texas. The blond, blue-eyed pitcher had a lightning-speed arm and a reputation as a bad boy.

He was also her father's favorite player, so Amanda knew him well, as did most women. The man was a walking sex god. Amanda didn't have to look too closely to decide he was even more of a hottie in person than on television.

Leaning all six feet of his rippling muscles against a locker, he fixed Amanda in a come-get-me stare. When he winked, she felt it all the way to her toes. The sizzle was instant. He made her burn. If she could pick any man to end her sexless existence, Brad would be the one. Too bad their jobs put him out of reach.

"Jack Ass fits him well most of the time," Brad drawled. "But we let him hang out, anyway."

"You can be a real ass yourself, Cowboy," Jack said in a biting tone and then shrugged. "And you let me hang around because I get you damn good press."

"Actually, it's all that free beer you buy us."

Jack's brow furrowed. "Say what you will, but we all know I deliver the readers." He looked at Amanda. "Unlike others."

"Since Jack got his face on the side of a bunch of buses and signs, he thinks he's important," Brad offered. "We know better."

Jack tuned Brad out, focusing on Amanda. "Do you know *anything* about baseball?"

Officially, Amanda was irritated. Jack had pushed far enough. Time to strike back. She laced her words with sticky sweet sarcasm. "You mean I need to understand baseball to do this job? Nobody told me that. Maybe you better start explaining it to me."

Laughter echoed against the tiled floors, boosting her confidence.

Numerous offers to school her on the art of baseball filled the air. Jack's expression soured until he looked as if he'd been sucking lemons. "Sweetheart, looking good will get you laid, but it ain't gonna get you a story."

She laughed, but inwardly the words stung, nestling amongst her insecurities that the only reason she had this job was because she looked good. She eyed Jack's slightly protruding belly and her response held more bite.

"Right. I most definitely do not want to look good. That makes me a very, very bad reporter. I should drink more beer and get me a body like yours. Then I'll get lots of stories." Amanda reached for her pad of paper and pen inside her purse. "I should take notes. What else do you think I need to know?"

More laughter filled the air. Jack's face reddened. "Funny. Real funny. We'll see who is laughing when your readership comes up a big zero."

She eyed her fingernails as if bored and then waved at Jack. "Bye-bye. Run along. I'm sure you have some major ego stroking to do." She turned her attention to Brad, offering Jack her back. "Great pitching today, by the way."

He grinned. "Thank you, ma'am."

"You've had two shutouts in a row, but there's speculation your old teammate, Mike Ackers, could rattle you next week. In fact, he promises a home run. What's your take on that?"

Brad eyed Jack with amusement evident in his expression, then motioned Amanda toward his open locker. "Well, darlin', why don't you step right over to my little home away from home, and let's talk about it."

She didn't have to look at Jack to know he was glaring. Amanda felt his stare like a dart landing in her back. Ah, but she liked it, relishing a little high from her successful verbal banter.

But the high shifted as she stepped close to Brad and his towel. Though she maintained a calm exterior, her heartbeat kicked into double time, pounding like a drum against her chest. The spicy scent of freshly showered male invaded her senses, and his gaze, direct and attentive, warmed her skin.

Amanda had met her share of professional athletes over the years, and none had affected her this way.

"So, ah, about those shutouts…" Amanda lost her

words as he reached down and made a slight adjustment to his towel. She followed the action with avid interest. She swallowed and forced her attention upward. "Maybe I should let you get dressed."

The corners of his full mouth lifted, mischief once again in his expression. "I trust you to shut your eyes if it falls off."

That made her laugh. She couldn't help it. No way in hell was she shutting her eyes if Brad Rogers lost his towel. He was lucky she didn't yank it off.

His eyebrow inched upward. "What's so funny?"

She shook her head, aware he was working her. "You're being very bad and you know it. You should cut the new girl a little slack."

"What fun is that?"

"Hey, reporter lady!"

Brad and Amanda both looked over to find Tony Rossi demanding her notice. An Italian with dark good looks and the best bat on the team, Tony had a reputation for playing the field with the ladies as much as he did the game.

"Her name is Amanda," Brad said.

Tony ignored him. "Why's he getting the first interview?"

She smiled, instantly taking a liking to Tony, possibly because of his directness. "I see you're competitive on and off the field," she teased. "I'll make sure you're next."

"Maybe I don't want to be next," he said, giving her the puppy dog eyes that only a player could deliver so effectively. "I get tired of being second to Brad."

Brad reached into his locker, pulled out a balled-up sock and threw it at Tony. "Shut up, man. What are you now? Twelve years old? Poor baby lost his place in line."

Amanda decided to toss a weapon of her own at Tony. "I hear that new pitcher, Rodriquez, has your number."

Tony's expression grew stormy, and he mumbled something in Italian that sounded fairly nasty. He poked at the air the way he did when he was yelling at the umpire, which tended to be far too often, and ended with a clear statement of, "That's bull."

One of the trainers called Tony's name, ordering him to the back room. Tony eyed Brad, ignoring the summons. "Tell her, man. Tell her it's crap." His gaze returned to Amanda. "I'm going to rip the seams off that asshole's ball. Print that. It's a quote."

"You can tell her when she's done with me," Brad said.

As Tony headed over to the trainer, Brad focused on Amanda. He rested one arm on top of the locker, framing her with his deliciously muscular body. "I need a favor," he said softly.

She stared at him and tried to figure out why he affected her so. Maybe it was his mouth. He had a full bottom lip, sensual and enticing. She could imagine how his mouth would feel pressed against her skin. Amanda blinked and resisted the urge to shake her head to rid it of the ridiculous thoughts.

"Favor?" she asked, a bit hoarsely. Delicately, she cleared her throat. "What would that be?"

"Before we go on…" He paused, leaning closer, his proximity wrapping her in sultry sensuality. A dart of electricity raced up her arm as his hand left the locker and settled on her elbow. Her entire body reacted, sending shivers along her nerve endings.

He tilted his head toward hers, his breath warm on

her neck as he whispered in her ear, "Promise you'll quote Tony." He eased backward to make eye contact. "He's very sensitive."

He might as well have asked her to get naked with him, because the impact of those words, the touch of his fingers against her bare skin and the heat of his body so near were nothing shy of sizzling.

"Tony is sensitive?" She found that hard to believe. "Mr. Macho?"

"The tough ones always are," he said. "Didn't you know that?"

Amanda laughed. Again. Suddenly, she realized how easily Brad amused her. And had her forgetting her work. Damn. She stiffened, reality taking hold. Brad could star in her nighttime fantasies, but that was it. Already the *Jack Ass* competition was questioning her talent and alluding to her being hired to seduce stories out of the players. The last thing she needed was to give those nasty speculations any basis in truth.

Raising her notepad, Amanda showed Brad what she had written. "Will rip the seams off the asshole's ball," she recited Tony's quote. "I might need to leave off the nasty names he used, though."

They shared a smile, the mutual attraction dancing in the air between them, but Amanda forced herself to be sober. She needed to get her interview with him, then move on before the other players slipped away.

She noticed the necklace around Brad's neck and a story idea formed. "A lucky charm?" she asked, knowing baseball players were the most superstitious of athletes, though she'd known a few football players who'd give them a run for their money.

His brow furrowed. "Lucky charm?"

"The necklace." She leaned closer, trying to see it again but pulled back to avoid another trip down lust lane. "Is that a Longhorn? As in, the University of Texas mascot?"

His hand went to the charm. "Yeah," he said. "My mom gave it to me on the day of my first college game." His serious expression was replaced by the cocky one he had been wearing. "I did a fine job of warming the bench to celebrate. My butt was downright smoking by the time I finally got a chance to prove myself."

What about his father? He hadn't said his parents had given him the necklace. Interesting... He had such a playboy image, hearing him talk about his mother surprised Amanda. Intrigued—from a strictly journalistic standpoint, of course—she wanted to know more. Fans gobbled up personal info about the players.

"You've done more than prove yourself since." She didn't mean her words as a compliment. They were simply a fact. During his twelve years in the majors, he'd become a near legend. Amanda didn't give him time to respond, her mind racing ahead with her story idea. "Have you worn the necklace all this time?"

He reached up and touched the charm again. "Every single day."

"So *is* it lucky?" Amanda asked. "Kind of like Michael Jordan's college shorts he wore beneath his game shorts?"

He shook his head and shut the locker, leaning against it as he crossed his arms in front of his nice, broad chest. "Oh, no," he said. "Don't go making me superstitious. You want superstitious, you want our center fielder."

Her mind scanned the roster she'd studied so intently before her job interview. "You mean Riley Walker?"

"Very impressive," Brad said. "I like a girl who does her homework."

She gave him a warning look, refusing to get pulled back into his flirtation. "Tell me about Riley."

He ran a hand over his stubble-darkened jaw. "He rubs some kind of oil on his glove before every game. One night he couldn't find it, and he had the entire team emptying their lockers searching for the damn stuff. It was pure craziness."

"What kind of oil? Like a leather lubricant?"

Brad shook his head. "Honestly, I don't know what the hell it is. Some peppermint-scented stuff. A Gypsy chick he dated in college fed him some junk about it creating a shield against bad omens. He really thinks he can't play without it."

Amanda could imagine the frayed tempers that must have been flying around the night of the missing magic oil. "Aren't you afraid I'll print this and make Riley mad?"

"I'm hoping you will." Brad grinned. "Bastard owes me two hundred bucks."

"I see," Amanda said, leaning against the closed locker beside his, wondering if the outstanding debt meant Riley had a gambling problem. "Surely, he has the money."

"Oh, he has the money," he said. "He just doesn't want to pay up."

Amanda accepted that answer…for now. Still, she scribbled a note about Riley. Couldn't hurt to see what his history looked like. She then needled Brad for a quote on the next week's game.

"Can you pitch a third shutout in a row?" she asked. "That would be your first."

"Only game day will answer that question, but I feel good. My arm is healthy. The team is strong." He lowered his voice. "Have drinks with me after the game, and I'll give you an exclusive."

Drinks. An exclusive. A hot kiss. Sounded good to her.

What didn't sound good, however, was risking her reputation. As good as he no doubt was, Brad Rogers was not worth compromising a career that had scarcely begun. Besides, there was his comment on his arm being healthy. It wasn't. She'd recognized the little signs of injury while he was on the field. The way he flexed his fingers. The way he discreetly rotated his shoulder. He had a weakness and he was hiding it. Why?

Sticking the pencil behind her ear, she managed to smile. "A tempting offer, but no." With true regret, she added, "I can't, and you know it."

His eyes narrowed on her face, his expression guarded but intense. "Too bad. Would have been fun."

"Yeah," she said, "but some things just can't be."

She paused, debating what to say to him, even as she told herself to walk away. But the truth was, his secret injury bothered her because she'd done the same thing. She'd pretended her knee was okay to pursue a shot at swimming in the Olympics. That choice had cost her her career.

Amanda waited until one of the players passed, then made sure her voice was low. "Ice that arm."

His eyes flashed with surprise. Surprise that told her she was right. When he said nothing, Amanda didn't know what to do. She started to leave, not sure she should have said anything.

His hand snaked out and shackled her wrist. She

rotated to face him. "I don't know what you're talking about," he said through gritted teeth.

She shrugged, not wanting to make him any tenser than he already was. "My father is an NFL team doctor and my sister is—"

"My arm is fine," he insisted, an edge to his tone this time.

"Okay," she said, but added in a whisper, "Ice it, Brad." She thought of all the things she'd heard her father say to players. The sooner he got his muscles nice and cold, the better. "Don't wait." Realizing where his thoughts must be going, she said, "This isn't about a story. I won't report it. You have my word."

He stared at her a moment, those blue eyes probing, looking for the truth, for proof he could trust her. Without another word, he let go of her and gave her a nod.

She left him then, but she felt his eyes on her. And, lord help her, it took every ounce of willpower to keep her attention from drifting to him. He'd earned a spot in her column for being so hot on the field.

He'd earned a spot in her fantasies for getting her so hot in the locker room.

2

AN HOUR AFTER meeting Amanda, Brad stood in the cleared-out locker room. He slammed his locker shut, ready to get the hell out of Dodge and find some ice for his aching arm. He was still reeling from the knowledge that Amanda had guessed he was injured. *Amanda*. A damn reporter, for God's sake. He was so screwed if word got out.

There was hope to cling to. Jack was cautious about what he printed, careful to keep his home team happy. With any luck, Amanda would use the same strategy.

"Got a minute, Rogers?"

Brad looked up to see Coach Locke standing in one of the trainer's doorways a few feet away. A fifty-something man with thick gray hair and a hard-as-nails exterior, he was tough but fair with his players and Brad respected him for that.

"Sure, Coach," Brad said, feeling tense when he normally wouldn't. With his contract up for renewal and his agent telling him to play it cool, Brad was more than a little on edge.

He wanted to stay in L.A. for what might very well be his last run around the bases. He'd moved his mother here last year when she'd had some health issues. She was doing well now, settled and happy, which meant relocation wasn't on his agenda. He wanted to bag five more years, hard and fast. Baseball was all he knew, and he wasn't ready to give it up yet.

Brad left his duffel bag on the bench and followed Coach into the tiny office. Coach sat behind the scuffed up wooden desk and Brad claimed the chair in front of him.

Coach tossed a newspaper at Brad. "Care to explain that?"

Brad cringed. The Ohio press had caught a picture of Brad and the rookie reliever Casey Becker in a heated debate at the airport. Damn it, this was so not what he needed right now. His agent had been preaching about Brad keeping a low profile. So much for that.

"I don't need to tell you this isn't the press you need."

"I know, Coach. I know." Thanks to a stupid bar fight almost a year ago, Brad had landed in the spotlight and in court. Unfortunately, the team owner had been dragged into the legal battle, as well.

"Do you know?" Coach challenged and jabbed at the paper. "It doesn't look like you know, to me."

"Becker is trouble and you know it. The kid has rocks in his head. He respects no one and doesn't listen to shit."

"I'm aware of the kid's attitude, but frankly, the owners are screaming about you, not Becker. I don't know if you're hoping to stay in L.A. or move on, but if you want to stay, this isn't the way to do it."

Brad's agent had cautioned him about seeming too eager. Mike thought that making the Rays believe Brad could walk away was critical to offset the prior year's fiasco. They'd argued the issue and Mike had won. After all, Mike Miller had been with him since day one of his career, and he'd never steered Brad wrong. He knew better than to second-guess Mike now, but damn it, he hated this. He wanted to sit down with the Rays and negotiate a new contract so he could focus on playing ball.

"I certainly want to keep my options open, Coach."

Coach narrowed his gaze on Brad, clearly not happy with that answer. "Well, this isn't the way to do it."

Brad told himself to bite his tongue but it bit his ass that the rookie had landed him in hot water. "Becker needs to be dealt with, Coach. If you don't get him in line, someone will. The kid's gonna get his balls busted if he doesn't show some respect to the veterans." And it was the truth. Rookies who came into The Show disrespecting the seasoned players eventually got what was coming to them.

"I know the kid is a royal pain, but right now we're talking about you. Keep your nose clean." Coach leaned back in his chair, rocking a minute. "You looked good tonight. How's that arm feeling?"

"Good," Brad lied. He'd followed that bar fight with surgery and the ensuing recovery time kept him off the mound and unable to show his value to the team. He needed to be on that field now, throwing strikes, and he knew it. Playing good ball would get him a contract renewal. "My arm feels good."

"Give me more of that heat you had on the mound tonight. Leave the rest at home."

Brad pushed to his feet. "I hear you, Coach."

Coach looked up at him, eyes narrowed in a scrutinizing stare. "I hope you do."

A FEW HOURS AFTER his meeting with Coach, and a long, rough talk with his agent later, Brad stood in the middle of the tiny Texas-style pool hall, beer in hand, music and smoke filtering through the air. A blue neon sign blinked on the wall behind him, and bottle caps lined the trim at the top of the walls. If he closed his ears to the Californian accents, he could almost believe he was back home. In front of him a game of pool was underway, several of his closest buddies competing.

Elbow resting on a round bar table, Brad wished like hell the pain inching from his wrist to his shoulder would go away. It throbbed and ached, a constant reminder he couldn't escape.

Just like his thoughts of Amanda. All that long auburn hair and those sultry curves served to distract him from his issues. But that was only part of it. She occupied prime space in his head because she knew his secret. She'd taken him from burning hot, ready to find a way to get her naked, to having a freaking heart attack with her caution to ice his arm. Man, if she—a journalist, for chrissake—figured it out, how long would it take his trainers and his coach to discover his secret?

A secret that was killing him.

After an hour of icing his arm and a double dose of ibuprofen, Brad had managed to drag himself to the traditional postgame festivities, also known as the postgame get-shit-faced gathering. Of course, Brad didn't do the shit-faced thing anymore. Not even on a night such as this one—the final night of a series followed by a few days off. The last time he'd had a few too many, he'd gotten in that damn bar fight and landed in a world of hurt with the press and the team. Of course, hitting a rich college kid whose father just happened to be a senator had certainly invited their wrath.

A beer bottle settled on the table with a loud thud,

jolting Brad out of his reverie. The offender was Kurt Caverns, the team catcher.

"I'm empty," Kurt announced and eyed Brad's bottle. "What's your status? Need a refill?"

Brad shook his head. "Nope. Not yet. Give me a few minutes, though, and I should be ready for another one."

"Saw you in Coach's office after the game," Kurt said, talking low, focused on Brad so no one else could hear. "Any word?"

Kurt referred to his contract. As Brad's closest friend, Kurt was the only one who knew how much he wanted to stay with the Rays and why. They'd both gone to University of Texas, though at different times. It had given them a bond that had opened the door to friendship. But even Kurt didn't know Brad's arm was hurting.

"The Ohio press got a shot of me and Becker arguing. Coach didn't like how it made me look."

"Damn, man, you can't live that fight down, can you?" He shook his head. "That freaking sucks."

"Yeah, it does," Brad said. "So does the timing."

"I've told Coach that Becker doesn't listen to jack," Kurt said. "I hate catching him. I give him a sign and he ignores it. And Coach is doing squat about it. He needs a hard lesson."

Brad had to agree. He had a damn good record on the mound, and the kid didn't have one at all. Yeah, Becker had talent but he was undisciplined and jeopardized as many games as he saved. He needed a lot of training, but he wasn't interested in receiving help. All that, and Brad was the one getting his ass chewed. Brad was the one with his career on the line. Because of a fight with a loudmouth University of Texas pitcher who reminded him a hell of a lot of Becker.

His agent had lectured him with more of the play-it-cool instructions tonight, but Brad wasn't feeling cool at all. He was feeling pretty damn hot, as a matter of fact. "Oh, I'd be happy to teach the kid a few lessons," he commented. "Doubt Coach would be happy, though."

"Probably not," Kurt agreed, "but Becker needs a reality check. Count me in on that play."

Determined to shake off his mood, Brad caught a glimpse of the pool table as Tony aimed his stick then made a horrific shot.

"Holy shit," Brad called out. "If I watch much more of this, I'll need two more beers and I'll need them fast." As if on cue, Tony scratched. Again. His third time that night. Brad tipped back his beer to hide a smile. Though Tony had been with the Rays only a year, he'd become part of the team almost instantly, not to mention fast friends with him and Kurt.

Brad watched in amazement as Tony proceeded to place the cue ball on the table as if he hadn't scratched. When Tony bent down to take another shot, Brad said, "Damn, Tony, if you're gonna cheat, do it well."

"Have you made even one shot tonight?" Kurt asked, adding insult to Tony's already wounded pride.

"Shut the hell up, Kurt," Tony snapped.

Kurt accepted a beer from a waitress who'd spotted his empty bottle. He gave her a wink and a tip before sauntering over to the table where he picked up the eight ball. "Good thing you swing the bat better than you play pool." He raised his beer. "I know. Maybe you need some luck. Why don't you get some of that peppermint oil Walker uses and rub it on your balls."

Brad laughed, almost spewing a mouthful of Bud.

"Shut up, Caverns." Tony's use of Kurt's last name indicated he was getting a serious attitude. "Before I shut you up."

"I'm scared, man. Truly shaking." Kurt nudged his ever present cowboy hat with his knuckle and fixed Tony with a speculative look. "You know what your problem is?"

Tony straightened, pool stick in his hand, irritation in his voice. "I'm sure you're going to tell me."

It was Brad's shot, but Tony's expression had him so amused he couldn't focus. Not only did Tony hate to lose, he was a sucker for a good verbal teardown over it. Kurt was always happy to oblige.

"You can't find the hole, man," Kurt said. "Guess that's why we haven't seen you with a woman in so long."

Tony rattled off a string of unpleasant words. "I get laid when I want to get laid."

Kurt laughed. "Right. The Italian Stallion you ain't."

"All you get are groupies. That doesn't make you the man." Tony bit the words out. "Anyone can score with them."

"Okay. Put your money where your mouth is." Kurt rubbed his palms together. "Let's make a bet. Pick a woman. Any woman. And let's see who can score first."

Tony leaned on his pool stick, a smile lifting the corner of his lips. "Okay." He motioned at Brad. "I see you laughing there, man. You aren't out of this. We bet. All three of us. And I know just the woman. The new reporter."

An instant *no* ripped through Brad's mind, and he barely kept it from sliding from his lips. Amanda was off-limits. Sure, she was hot. She damn sure got *him* hot. But it didn't matter. She, or more accurately her job, was trouble with a capital T. The kind that could screw up the career he was desperately trying to hang on to. The wrong thing said across the pillows and he could wave a contract renewal goodbye.

"Don't mess with the press," he said. "Pick another woman."

Tony waved off the warning. "She won't report her own indiscretions."

"But she can twist them in her favor," Brad countered. "She has the pen and the audience." He paused, his lips thinning as he remembered his own personal media bashing. "We all know what happened to me."

Kurt chimed in. "You know what they say about female reporters?" He didn't wait for an answer. "Once she gets you to drop your pants, she'll bend you over."

Tony grinned. "I'll do her so right she'll want to brag to the world."

"I hear that," Kurt said, as he flagged a waitress and pointed to Brad's empty bottle, taking the liberty to order for him. "But she's still trouble, man."

Grabbing the opening Kurt had given him, Brad eyed the blond hottie tending bar. "Forget the reporter," he said and used his chin to motion toward the suggested target. "How about her?"

Tony broke out in a smile, pointing at Brad. "I know what's up. I figured you out. You already tried with the reporter and got shut down. You know you can't win this bet."

"She busted your chops, didn't she?"

The voice from behind Brad was distinct and all too familiar. A New York accent delivering a smart-ass comment could only be the rookie—Brad's nemesis of the past few months.

Becker came into view, his pressed Dockers and

collared shirt looking more preppy than cowboy. Even his blond hair was perfectly groomed—buzzed on the sides, longer on the top, maybe a hint of hair product to hold it in place. He looked like Mr. *GQ*. He *always* looked like Mr. *GQ*.

"Becker," Brad said, giving him a nod.

"Hey, old man."

Brad shook his head at the tired jab, wondering if the kid would ever grow up, or at least get new material. "What brings you out tonight?"

Becker lifted his draft beer—figured. The kid couldn't even drink beer like a man, he had to sip from a glass. "Same as you, I suspect. A little celebration. A little drinking." He paused. "That reporter from the *Tribune*…I saw you try to score with her." Becker flashed his perfect white smile. "She shut you down."

"You don't know what you're talking about, kid," Brad said, refraining from making a much snider remark and taking a slug of beer. "If I wanted her, I could have her."

"She's not your type," Becker said. "She's what you call a *lady*." He leaned on the pool table. "And a lady needs a certain kind of man."

"What the hell does that mean?" Brad demanded, feeling the rise of his temper. The comment bit his ass, and it bit hard.

"You can hand a good ol' boy money, but you can't teach him about being a gentleman," Becker said. His gaze was insolent as he eyed Brad's faded Levi's with obvious meaning.

Inhaling deeply, Brad managed to keep his sour words to himself. Not an easy task, considering the sorry little bastard not only had landed him in hot water today, but basically had insulted his mother. A mother who'd worked her backside off on a teacher's salary to help Brad achieve his dreams, who'd kept him striving even after his dad had died during his junior year of high school.

But if he was honest with himself, the thought of Amanda with Becker didn't sit well. The idea of that punk touching her, taking her, when Brad wanted her, brought a bitter taste to his mouth. If anyone on this team was getting Amanda naked, damn it, it was going to be him.

"You think Amanda, or any woman for that matter, wants a snotty nosed little boy?" Brad asked, then followed with a disbelieving sound. "She'd be screaming my name long before you could even find her bra strap."

Becker's face started to redden as he clenched his jaw. "Say what you will, old man," he replied in a tight voice. "Talk is cheap."

Tony pounded a fist on the pool table. "Now this is a bet I am in on for sure."

Kurt spoke up then, clearly having realized why this was not a good idea. "Brad's right. The shit'll hit the fan if Coach hears you're screwing with the press."

"I like the press," Becker said with a gloating look in Brad's direction. "And they like me."

Brad ground his teeth together. Despite Coach's warnings to leave Becker alone, Brad wanted nothing more than to teach the kid a lesson in respect. "Fine, kid. You got yourself a bet." He might regret this, but his pride had taken enough for one night.

Without giving Becker—or anyone else—a chance to respond, Brad walked away. The bet was made and once he'd committed to a play, he took it all the way.

Amanda would be his soon, and keeping the new reporter occupied might be a good idea. He'd give her something other than his arm to think about.

3

TO CELEBRATE her first foray into the Rays' locker room, Amanda shared dinner with her assigned photographer, Reggie Sheldon. Considering she'd only met him that morning, Amanda was surprised she already felt comfortable with him. He'd guided her through what could have been a rough first day of work, and helped her make sense of all the new people and places. The hole-in-the-wall restaurant he had sworn she'd enjoy had indeed been an exceptional choice. The food was phenomenal.

Amanda tossed her napkin on the tiny square table and sighed. "You were right," she admitted. "That was great Mexican food. I thought for sure I'd given up such fare when I left Texas."

"Told you," Reggie said, pushing his empty plate aside. "Los Angeles is the other Texas."

Amanda laughed. "Not sure what that means but okay."

"L.A. is a melting pot. There is so much diversity here. It keeps things interesting."

Reggie himself seemed to be a melting pot of characteristics. A heavyset black man with dreadlocks and stern features, his forearm sported a tattoo of Mickey Mouse. She was coming to know his choice of tattoo matched his unexpected sense of humor.

"*Interesting* is moving in a matter of days," Amanda commented. "I still can't believe this time two weeks ago I didn't even know I was moving. I've started working before most of my wardrobe even crossed the state line." She glanced at her watch. "Wow. It's late. I have to write up something about tonight's game for tomorrow's paper."

"That's just a quick write-up, at least. It's a good way to get your feet wet. The real pressure, I imagine, is your first feature."

"Oh, yeah." Butterflies fluttered in her stomach thinking about submitting that feature. "It's not due until Monday night, so I have three days to fret about what to write."

"I have a feeling you'll do just fine," he assured her. "But I better get you home to write tomorrow's piece."

"You mean my hotel?" she asked, but she didn't give him time to respond, her mind on the work ahead of her. "Speaking of my story, did you get any shots of that home run Tony hit?"

"The one he blasted halfway to Texas?" Disbelief laced his tone. "What kind of wingman would I be if I missed that kind of shot?"

"Wingman, huh?" She kind of liked the sound of that. Back in Dallas, she'd been lucky to have her own coffee mug, let alone a wingman.

"That's right, honey cakes." He gave her a nod. "The right arm to your left. The holder of thy hand in troubled times."

"Honey cakes?"

"What?" He lifted his eyebrow. "You don't like your new nickname?"

"I guess you don't like Amanda?"

"Amanda is a fine name."

When he said nothing else, she took the bait. "But?"

He shrugged. "It's what everyone else calls you. I don't like being like everyone else."

"You're joking right?" she asked. "Using my name *would* make you different. The players called me every name imaginable but Amanda. *Honey. Baby. Sweetie.*" She rolled her eyes. "Men." Then quickly added, "Present company excluded, of course."

They paid the bill, then left the restaurant.

"What do you know about Jack?" Amanda asked, as they settled into the van.

"Jack Ass?" Reggie asked. "I mean Krass." He started the ignition. "I guess I should have warned you about him."

"Ya think? Seems a wingman's duty if I ever heard of one."

"Yeah, well, I hate to waste good air talking about that sorry bastard."

"I take it you don't like him any more than I do," she commented. "So what's the story?"

"In a nutshell," he said, maneuvering the van onto the highway, "he's an asshole."

"And a chauvinist bastard. He treated me like I didn't know sports because I'm a woman."

"Jack lashes out when he feels threatened."

"He didn't act threatened."

"Oh, he's threatened. Kevin finally got smart about who he hired to replace star Jack. You have an advantage over the two guys before you, and Jack knows it."

"And what exactly would that advantage be? Because I have to tell you, I didn't feel any advantages back there in that locker room."

Reggie cast her a sideways look. "A woman has an edge when it comes to men. You can get guys to admit to and talk about stuff they won't with other guys. What you do with that edge is what counts. And right now, Jack knows you are getting attention he wants as his own."

Amanda digested that information in silence. She'd never considered being female as one of the reasons she was good at her job. But then, it wasn't until after her makeover that she'd started to see her feminine assets.

Still, her gender couldn't completely explain Jack's reaction to her. "Jack seems pretty tight with the Rays. Don't get me wrong, they gave him a hard time. But it was in a you're-one-of-the-guys kind of way. When we were in the other team's locker room, not so much. But with the Rays, he was the one who seemed to have the edge."

"He's been around a long time." They pulled up to a stoplight and Reggie gave her his full attention. "When he first started with the paper, he seemed real down-to-earth. A good guy. He was eager to earn the players' trust—always printing their side of the story while still being objective. And the team takes care of their own. Jack ended up with all kinds of exclusives." His lips thinned. "And that's when the real Jack showed his colors. He changed in a big way. One minute, a nice guy. The next, cocky and demanding. The bigger his readership, the bigger his head."

"And the players?" Amanda prodded. "Did they notice?"

"Oh, yeah, they noticed. But he was inside their circle. He'd looked the other way on some things, didn't oversensationalize some career-damaging incidents, so the team hung tight. Until Jack does someone dirty, the guys won't kick him out. But let me tell you, he will.

Jack's new job is a stepping stone to bigger things. He's going to do what it takes to get to the next level."

From the conviction in Reggie's words, she knew he had experienced the bad side of Jack firsthand. "Jack did you dirty."

The light turned green and Reggie focused on the road. "When we worked together he talked a lot about the two musketeers. All for one and one for all." Pause. "In the end, Jack was out for Jack."

"He burned you pretty bad, huh?"

Reggie didn't look at her. "I let it happen," he said and didn't elaborate.

Amanda wanted to push him for details but decided it was best she leave it alone. They'd only just met, and Reggie had no reason to trust her. But in time, maybe he'd feel he could tell her the entire story.

"After being burned by Jack, I'm surprised you're so willing to be my wingman."

He laughed, but not with humor. In fact, the sound rang with a hint of bitterness. "*Because* of Jack, I'm willing to be your wingman." He cast her a sideways glance and winked. "I want to see him go down, and I've a good feeling you can kick some Jack Ass. In fact, I'm counting on it."

"You and me both," she murmured, feeling the pressure of success more than ever.

She'd known her predecessor would be tough competition. Now, she knew Jack was more than that. If he would stoop to such low levels to achieve success, even burn those closest to him, he'd certainly bury her, given the chance.

But Jack Krass wasn't standing between her and success—and she refused to let him. He reminded her of her ex, who'd been willing to do anything to get ahead, even marry her. Though she'd put her marriage behind her, she had learned to be wary of people like her ex, like Jack.

She wouldn't play dirty the way Jack did. She'd play smart. And she would prove good reporting and good ethics could defeat big egos and dirty deeds every time.

BY MONDAY NIGHT, Amanda had written and rewritten her first feature story so many times, she wanted to rip her hair out. Now as she stared at the blank screen of her notebook computer, the pressure of that short time frame she had to capture an audience had her second-guessing herself.

One angle played over and over in her mind. If being a woman gave her an edge, why not use that edge in her column? How could she translate that advantage to the page in a way that connected with readers? She toyed with the hem of her oversize T-shirt while she considered and discarded potential story threads. As seemed typical since meeting him, her thoughts strayed to images of Brad wearing that skimpy towel. In her fantasies, a bolder version of herself tugged off that towel and indulged her every sensual impulse in the perfection of his body. Maybe she should make him the focus of her feature, write this crazy urge out of her system.

Her cell started to shake on the bedside table, disrupting her thoughts. Eying the caller ID, Amanda wasn't surprised to see her sister's number. She put the receiver to her ear, and before she could even speak, the verbal barrage started.

"You didn't call me," Kelli reprimanded. "It's been days and not one phone call. How am I supposed to know what's going on if you don't phone?"

Amanda leaned against the headboard, preparing for a long chat. "Hello to you, too."

"Screw hello. I've used great restraint not calling before now. I want the gossip. Tell me everything. How did the first night go?"

"I didn't trip and fall, and my skirt did not get stuck in my panty hose. I'd say it was a success."

"Falling isn't so bad. Nothing wrong with creating opportunity for chivalry."

Amanda remembered all too well her tumbling act, smack in the middle of the food court at the mall, when she'd switched from flats to heels. "Preferably not when landing facedown, looking like a fool, I would assume."

"You didn't look like a fool." Kelli gave an unladylike snort. "Okay, a little, but it was your first day in heels."

"I still can't believe I fell," Amanda said. "I never do stuff like that."

"Walking like a goddess in heels is an art."

"So I found out," Amanda agreed. "I'm just waiting for the toe-pinching to subside."

"You get used to that, too."

"One day I might grow up and be a diva doctor like you," Amanda teased.

"You could never be a doctor. You turn blue at the sight of blood. Besides, my dear little sis, why would you want to develop a God complex? Doctors, pilots and athletes all have gargantuan egos and you are much too sweet to either acquire one or date one."

"Diva doctors are much better than God complex doctors," Amanda replied dryly. Her sister had reason to be a bit cocky, since she was one of the best sport medicine doctors in Dallas, possibly in Texas.

"You don't see me running off getting married," Kelli said, not disputing her diva status one bit.

"No, you certainly are not. No marriage for you. I've heard it a million times." Amanda mimicked her sister, "All play and no stay."

Kelli wasn't fazed. "Speaking of play, how 'bout them ballplayers?"

A smile lifted Amanda's lips as she thought again of Brad's towel. "I don't remember the locker rooms being so—"

"Hot?" Kelli asked. "Heck, yes. There is enough beefcake in the locker room to keep a girl drooling for hours. You were so freaked out by the blood, you stopped hanging out with the guys before you were old enough to enjoy the scenery." She made an unladylike sound. "Well, that and the fact you were talking like a sailor. It was quite comical. Cute little thing until you opened your mouth."

"Well, I'm enjoying it now and, believe it or not, my sailor talking past comes in handy these days."

"Just don't go falling for one of those beefcakes."

"Daddy's a doctor." Surely their father proved the exception to Kelli's God complex rule.

"And Mom is a saint." Apparently not. "Which reminds me. Call Mom and Dad. They are freaking out worrying that their little baby is okay."

Amanda rolled her eyes. "Good grief. I've only been gone a few days. I'm twenty-eight and divorced, not eighteen and headed off to college."

"That's Mom and Dad. You know how they worry."

"I'll call," Amanda promised. "But I have to make my deadline first."

"How's that going?"

"Not good." Amanda went on to explain her run-in with her competition. "I'm thinking the best way to fight him is by embracing the whole woman power thing. Maybe try to draw female readers who might not otherwise even open the sports section."

"Hmm," Kelli said, pondering. "I like the concept but how do you do that and write a sports column?"

"What if my column could be the *Cosmopolitan* of sports? You know, take the personal side of the athletes, and blend it with their performance on the field."

"I'm not following."

"Well, I found out about a lot of superstitious stuff the guys do before the games. It gave me an idea about sharing the secrets behind the players. Digging into the men behind the uniform. I could top it off with suggestions for a sexy headline."

"I like it. You have to have the game stats, though."

"Right. But after the rundown, I'll highlight a player's more personal side. I was thinking I'd start with Brad Rogers."

Kelli made a purring sound. "Good place to start. *Yu-m-m-y.* Oh crap. I have to go. I have a date in ten minutes, and I still haven't fixed my hair. But I love your idea. And don't forget to take your vitamins. Kisses."

The line went dead.

Amanda rolled her eyes as she punched the End button and dropped her phone on the bed. Her sister was an herbal supplement freak, which made absolutely no sense, since most doctors hated them. But then, her sister wasn't what anyone expected a doctor to be. She was as unique as they came.

Speaking of unique, Amanda had a kick-ass article to write. A kick-ass article featuring Brad…

She sighed, and leaned against the headboard, giving herself a few minutes to consider how hot he'd gotten her. After two years of being single and pretty damn close to celibate, she'd started to think her On switch had been locked in the Off position. Thanks to Brad, she knew not only was she on, but she was downright smoking.

Her mind pictured those rippling abs. The trail of blond hair starting at his navel and disappearing beneath the towel. She so wanted to see where it ended.

Yet, if she found out, if she dared to get lost in those sultry blue eyes, to taste those full, sensual lips, she knew how that would look. No one would take her seriously and it would be impossible to do her job. She would have to pack and go home. Any success she might have would be wiped away, dismissed as part of her bedroom antics.

Regret settled in her stomach. It had been so long since she'd felt this fire of attraction, this desire for physical satisfaction, and her libido had chosen a man out of reach. The only place she could have Brad was in a fantasy.

Maybe a little trip down fantasy lane was what the doctor ordered. A little mental satisfaction would rid her of this restless sensation. Amanda's lashes fluttered, and she inhaled, allowing the sensual tension to flare.

What would sex with Brad be like?

Her hands settled on her stomach as she visualized him lying beside her, sprawled naked on the bed, sinewy muscles glistening in the candlelit room. He'd be hard for her, ready for her to take him inside her. But she wouldn't give him what he wanted. Not at first. She'd take control, tease him, make him wait and want.

She'd climb on top of him, straddle him, his cock

pressed to her backside. She might even reach behind her and stroke its length.

Her hands traveled over her body. She'd touch herself as he watched, tempting him without allowing him to caress her. She slid deeper into the imagined feel of naked skin against naked skin. Amanda palmed her breasts and her nipples puckered and tingled as she thought of Brad's gaze, of his hunger as he watched her pleasure herself. He'd try to pull her close, to take control, and she'd shove his hands away, warning him not to touch…not until she said he could. Not until she gave permission. *Yes.* Dominating a man so wholly male was enticing. Exciting.

She'd lean forward, her nipples brushing his chest, nestled for a moment in the soft sprinkle of light brown hair there. From beneath a pillow, she'd produce the tools to ensure his compliance, two long silk scarves. She'd watch her intent register in his eyes, see his conflict as he debated resisting. But in the end, he'd let her tie him up. He'd hand over his power. And he'd be rewarded….

Taking her time, Amanda would secure his wrists, one by one. Her nipple would brush his lips and he'd claim it with his lips, pulling it into his mouth, suckling the hardened peak. Just thinking of that moment made her body ache, made her wet with desire.

When she'd secured him, when Brad was her prisoner, she'd begin the real game. She'd move between his powerful thighs, his cock hard, her hand circling its width. And she'd watch him watch her as she drew him into her mouth. Watch his eyes shut as he took a breath of pure pleasure.

Amanda thought of all the ways she could tease and

please him. Her fingers slid between her legs, into the wet heat of her body, images of a new scene with Brad taking hold. Images of climbing on top of him, of taking him deep. Of riding him until she shattered with release.

Driving herself wild with desire, she felt the throbbing pressure of her orgasm build until, finally, she found release. And with release came regret that, as much as she wanted to, she could never dare to do these things to him, with him, outside of this fantasy.

4

BRAD WOKE Tuesday morning to the ringing of the phone on his nightstand. He rolled over to check the time. Early. Seven in the morning on one of the few days he could sleep in, since their series didn't start until the next night. With a groan he grabbed the receiver.

"Have you seen the morning edition of the *Tribune?*"

It was his agent, Mike. "No." Brad pushed to a sitting position, instantly alert. *Please don't let it be about my arm.* "Do I want to?"

"Oh, yeah," Mike said. "You want to. It's good stuff. Exactly what we need for this negotiation. Read it. Like it. Thank God for it after that Ohio piece. Give me more stuff like this and you'll lock up that contract in no time."

Brad threw off the blankets and grabbed a robe before heading toward his front door. Though it didn't sound as if the news was about his arm, he wouldn't be calm until he knew for sure.

Brad prodded for more information, hoping to ease his nerves. "What exactly did it say?"

"The *Tribune* did an exposé titled, *Undressing the Rays* and you were the feature. Brad Rogers stripped down to a good guy who loves his mom. Man, oh man. It couldn't get better than this if I had bribed the reporter."

Brad could hear Mike rustling papers. "Now we need that record. Ready to rock the world tonight?"

"Not tonight. Friday night. And I was born ready. You know that." But even as Brad said the words, he knew he wasn't ready. Already his arm hurt and he'd just woken up.

"That's what I want to hear," Mike said, approval lifting his voice. "Bring me three shutouts in a row. That'll go a long way in negotiations."

"Right." Brad yanked open the front door and grabbed both morning papers. "Good press. Great pitching. No problem." Hopefully his arm agreed with that declaration.

After a quick goodbye, Brad kicked the front door shut and headed for the kitchen. He sat at the table and read the piece Amanda had written about him, breathing easier with each line.

No mention of his arm.

With one worry behind him, his mind switched gears. This article gave Brad the perfect opportunity to make his move on Amanda, to open the door to more intimate communication. He considered his options, a variety of rather tantalizing plays to launch his campaign to victory flashing in his mind. Soon Becker would know who ruled this show. And who was man enough to make Amanda moan.

ON TUESDAY MORNING, the day of her column's debut, Amanda whipped her piece-of-junk rental car into a parking spot outside the *Tribune* with only minutes to spare. How she'd managed to snag a rental that seemed on the verge of a breakdown was beyond her. The last thing she needed was to be late for work only a few days into her new job. Of course, it might not matter. She could very well be fired after writing such a daring story.

She'd hit the Send button on her computer the night before, delivering her story to her boss just in time to meet her deadline. Afterward, Amanda had stared at her inbox waiting to hear his feedback. It never came.

This morning, having slept through her alarm, Amanda had been forced to dress in a frantic rush, leaving her no time to find a newspaper. For all she knew, some Associated Press filler had taken her story's place.

Shoving aside self-doubt, Amanda walked toward the building, running her palm down the slim-fitting black dress she wore, hoping she didn't appear wrinkled. She knew she was fidgeting so she wouldn't focus on the nerves making her chest tight and her stomach flutter.

She'd done the right thing, she told herself. Considering the short window of opportunity she'd been given to succeed, she had to make a splash, and fast. Adopting the Nike motto of Just Do It had worked in the pool. It could work here, too.

Amanda walked through the newsroom, turning heads and instigating hushed whispers as she passed. Great. Everyone but her knew she was getting fired. She let out a relieved sigh at the sight of her boss's closed door. She preferred seeing the paper before she faced Kevin.

But all her fears and concerns disappeared as Amanda stepped inside her tiny corner cubicle and spotted the front page of the sports section laid on her keyboard. She picked it up and stared down at story center page. *Her* story.

Undressing the Los Angeles Rays. Beneath the racy

headline, she saw her name. Beneath that, the words *staff writer.* A smile touched Amanda's lips. She wasn't a flunky anymore and, damn, it felt good.

"Whatcha think, sugar plum?"

Reggie appeared in the opening of her little space. "I think I'm a ball of nerves," she told him, examining the rows of thumbnail pictures on either side of her story. "And you're my hero." She'd asked him to dig up photos that showed Brad on and off the field, and he'd come through. "I can't believe what great shots you found."

He flashed her a bright white smile. "That's what a wingman is for."

"So…what did you think about the story?" she asked, anxious to hear but afraid to at the same time. So much so, she continued talking before he could respond. "I went for a dual audience. Draw in the men with the facts. Entice the women with the real man and a promise of lots more to come."

"Stop already," Reggie said, leaning on the wall. "You scored big-time. You've got just enough sports to keep it real, but you've got that edgy, speculative quality that sells papers."

She bit her bottom lip. "So as a guy, you'd still read it? You weren't turned off by the real man stuff."

He shook his head. "Actually, as a guy, I loved the part about Brad's lucky necklace. It made him seem human. Besides, men are all about superstition when it comes to our sports. It's something a guy could relate to."

Before Amanda could comment, Kevin appeared, resting his arms on the top of her partition walls. The shininess of her boss's bald head did nothing to detract from the scowl on his face—the one he'd worn in her interview that she would have sworn meant he hated her.

"My phone is ringing off the hook," he declared, his tone clipped and rough.

Amanda and Reggie exchanged a concerned look. "About?" she prodded because Kevin seemed to expect her to ask the obvious.

"Some of the players are worried about your promise to expose the real men."

Reggie made a sound. "Then they must have something to hide. Sounds like news to me."

Kevin didn't say anything. He stared at her, ignoring Reggie. Amanda's heart settled in her chest and proceeded to beat so loudly she was quite certain the entire building could hear. "Right. I—"

Kevin cut her off. "The papers are flying off the racks." Then, to her shock, he smiled. Almost. His lips sort of lifted on the sides a bit. She doubted the man ever full-out smiled. "You need to ease up a little. I printed the story, so obviously, I thought it worked. Every newspaperman worth a grain of salt knows sex and scandal sells. Good work."

Amanda blinked, taken aback and thrilled by the compliment. "I, uh, well, thank you."

"Speaking of 'Undressing the Rays,' there's a rumor of steroid usage on the team. Jack's working the story."

Steroids? That was the kind of story that ruffled feathers. The kind of story one treaded lightly around. The wrong information could ruin careers. "Do I get to know your source?"

"No." His tone was clipped. "I've been around a long time. I've earned my contacts. You haven't yet. All you need to concern yourself with is getting this story before Jack. Understand?"

Her response was instant. "Oh, yes. I want that, too." Amanda made sure her voice held the conviction she felt.

Kevin's eyebrow inched upward, but he didn't comment. "Good. I expect an update soon." Without another word, he left.

Hand pressed to her chest, Amanda felt both relieved and happy. "Oh, my God, I just knew I was getting fired."

"You scored big," Reggie told her. "Now you have nothing to worry about except—"

"Getting this story before Jack Ass."

"Right," he said with a nod. "But don't fixate on Jack. Do this your way, not his. And that wasn't what I was going to say, anyway. I was going to say you need to find a place to live."

"Oh," Amanda said, settling into her chair. "I know. Kevin said to get here, so that's what I did. I need time to find something I can afford. So far, everything the real estate agent has showed me is crazy expensive or so far away it's nuts."

"I might have a solution," Reggie offered. "Karen Tuggle, our weather woman, has a duplex and she rents out the other side. I'm not sure when it's available, but it's in a good area of town and it's affordable."

"Sounds good. I'll contact her today. I'm hoping Kevin lets me travel with the team for the Texas series in six weeks. That way I can drive my own car back."

"I'd bet on it. The Rangers and the Rays have a competitive history with some tension between the coaches. Jack Ass will be going for sure. All the more reason for Kevin to want us there."

Amanda's cell phone rang before she could respond.

"I'll check in with you in a bit," Reggie said, before departing.

Amanda managed to retrieve her phone from her purse by the third ring. Caller ID told her it was her father. "Hey, Dad."

"How is my baby girl?"

"I'm fine." Amanda smiled into the phone. "My first story hit the paper today."

"I saw that," he said, his voice holding a fatherly authoritative tone as if he wasn't completely pleased his daughter had written it. "And quite the story it was. I bet you got some notice."

"I did," Amanda agreed. "And the good news is, I'm still employed."

"Well, of course you are. But let me get this straight. You wrote the article thinking it might cost you your job?"

"No." She blinked. "Well, maybe. It *is* a bit daring," Amanda admitted.

"You certainly made everyone sit up and take notice, and you did it right out of the gate." He paused. "I noticed you picked Brad Rogers as your first feature, too."

"I knew you'd approve." Her father had a thing for pitchers. Not teams, but pitchers. Brad was a favorite. Amanda loved watching baseball with her highly opinionated father. Just listening to him complain about the bad calls, bad pitching, bad coaching and a long list of other *bad* things, kept her entertained.

"You didn't happen to get—"

She rolled her eyes. "No, Daddy, I did not get you an autograph. Give me time to be accepted."

A heavy sigh filled the phone. "All right, but don't wait too long. You know how I like my autographs."

"Yes," she said, thinking of his den filled with his collection. "I do know. I'll get you one. I promise."

"Before he quits pitching."

She frowned. "You think he's going somewhere?"

"He's playing hurt. You know from your own history what that means."

She knew very well. "I noticed, too. He kept doing that little flexing movement between pitches. Discreet, but obvious if you're a doctor."

"Or the daughter of one," her father said.

"I couldn't listen to you and Kelli talk shop and not pick up something. The odd thing is that no one with the Rays seems to have noticed that Brad's hurt. I noticed, but not them. How crazy is that?"

"You've been in the locker rooms. Broken bones and blood get attention. The rest is easy to miss. Especially when it's being hidden." A female voice sounded in the background. "Hold on," he said. "I have lots more to ask, but your mother feels it's her time to talk. Love you, honey."

"Love you, too, Daddy."

"Don't forget my autograph."

She laughed. "I'll get it."

"Oh," he said, as if he'd had a last-minute thought. "Any word on you coming home for the Texas series?"

"Not yet," Amanda said, feeling the pressure of performance. The team would head to Nashville before Texas, and she didn't know about that trip. "I imagine that decision will come once they decide if I'm a keeper or not."

"Then I'll see you soon," he said, confident in her as always.

Amanda chatted with her mother a few minutes and

then hung up. She was forever grateful for her parents' confidence and support.

It was time to earn that confidence. She was going to find the story behind every teeny-weensy towel in that locker room…even if she wasn't allowed to remove any of them.

LATE FRIDAY AFTERNOON, Amanda sat at her desk jotting down potential interview questions for the locker room postgame, nerves working a number on her stomach. She had a lot of ground to cover. Tuesday's game had gone so horribly for the Rays that the coach had shut the locker room to the press. Wednesday and Thursday had been off nights so there'd been no talking with the players for her second column. She'd gone with Riley's Gypsy oil as her featured superstition but hadn't gotten as deep into the topic as she would have liked. Tonight would be her first chance to find out Brad's reaction to her story on him.

Brad.

He'd stayed on her mind far too much.

A loud thud jerked Amanda to attention. Kevin stood in front of her cubicle, having tossed two big bags on the floor. He pointed to one. "Fan mail." Then to the other. "Hate mail."

Amanda gulped. "Hate mail?"

"Attention is attention," Kevin said. "Think Howard Stern. Keep this up and you might actually stay around a while."

She couldn't quite get past the hate mail. "Why do they hate me?"

Irritation flashed in his face. "It doesn't matter. What matters is that you get that steroid story before Jack.

Check out Tony Rossi. My source says Jack thinks he's the user. My question to you is why does Jack know this and you don't?"

"I—"

"I want that story, Amanda. Whatever it takes, get it."

She was being asked to earn the team's trust and destroy a player's career all at once. It seemed as wrong as the hate mail. She'd signed up to be a reporter, not a destroyer.

"And another thing," Kevin continued. "The team's headed to Nashville. Jack's not, so you're not. That damn hotel room of yours is eating up my budget. Get a place to live before I find one for you."

He wanted her to get the story, but he wasn't letting her go with the team. That didn't make sense. Shouldn't she go because Jack wasn't going? Wouldn't that give her an edge?

She bit her tongue and focused on the solution she could give him. "I'm renting from Karen Tuggle. I move in next week."

"Good. And how much longer do you have that rental car?"

She reminded him of their interview conversation. "We discussed me taking a few days after the Texas series to drive mine back."

He grunted. "That's several more weeks."

His attitude was getting to her. They'd agreed to these terms before she'd started. "With the company discount, the rental came out cheaper than the cost to transport my car here."

Reggie appeared. "Ready to hit the road?"

Amanda pushed to her feet. "I'm ready."

Kevin fixed her with a level stare. "Get me that

story," he ordered before exiting, leaving her staring after him, feeling frazzled.

The phone on her desk rang and Reggie motioned toward the door. "I'll meet you downstairs."

She waved, sitting back down and reaching for the phone. "This is Amanda."

"This is the star of your first column at the *Tribune*."

Her heart beat like a drum in her chest. "I never had the chance to ask what you thought of it. Did you like it?" she asked.

"I told you not to make me out to be superstitious," he reminded her, but his voice held no anger. In fact, his tone seemed flirtatious.

"I didn't," Amanda said. "I made you out to be sentimental. And the way I see it, I did you a favor."

"A favor, huh? What exactly was the favor?"

"Well," she drawled, picking up a pencil and tapping it on the desk, needing an outlet for the adrenaline coursing through her body. "You've had some bad press, what with the fight and being out for part of the season. The public needed a reminder that you may be more good ol' boy than bad boy. I suspect your team did, as well."

"My agent agrees with you on that point, even if I don't see it. I guess I'll cut you some slack on the superstition thing."

"So kind of you. I was worried. Really, I was."

"You really are a good smart-ass. I noticed that when you talked to Jack."

"Jack," she said, her lips thinning with the name. "Such a nice guy."

Brad let out a bark of laughter. "Right. I could see how well you two got along. Now, back to the article and my thoughts on it. You left some unanswered questions. It felt a bit unfinished."

She frowned. "What unanswered questions?"

"Who is the real man behind the ballplayer?" he recited the question she'd posed in her story.

"It wasn't meant as a literal question," she replied, wishing like hell she could answer it herself first-hand. Wondering why she wanted to so badly. She didn't get distracted by such things. "It was meant to pique interest."

"I think you owe it to your readers to find out."

"Oh, really?" she said, forgetting Kevin and that hate mail. "I got the impression you wanted the 'real man' kept private."

"Depends on who's involved," he said, his tone low, suggestive.

"You're offering me an interview?"

"That's right. Tonight. After the game." He paused. "Strictly business, of course."

If it was *strictly business,* why say so? "Of course," she agreed, though she sensed there was more than that going on between them. And, damn it to hell, her fantasy image of him, gloriously naked and tied to her bed, chose that moment to flash in her mind.

"Goodbye, Amanda."

She blinked away the erotic images, reprimanding herself for allowing them to surface. "Goodbye, Brad."

The line was silent a moment, neither of them hanging up, their breathing soft, intimate, sizzling with promise. Amanda forced herself to set the receiver on the cradle.

What had just happened? She grabbed a piece of paper and fanned herself. She'd never been this tempted to stray from a goal. And her career represented an important goal. Yet, Brad had most definitely proven he could seize her attention and make her forget all the reasons she needed to avoid him. If the man could get her this hot on the phone, what could he do in person?

And there was the question she couldn't help but want answered. Yet, she couldn't—no, wouldn't—allow herself to find out. Brad Rogers was off limits. She wasn't about to compromise her journalistic integrity to discover if some ballplayer with a God complex burned up the sheets as much as his voice promised.

She pushed to her feet, and made herself repeat her vow. She would not be seduced by Brad Rogers.

And that was that.

She hoped.

5

SEVERAL HOURS AFTER Amanda's little chat with Brad on the phone, she walked to the ballpark concession stand, Reggie by her side. "You enjoy your talk with the girls?" he asked.

"Actually, I did," Amanda said, surprised at how much she'd learned from her powwow with some of the groupies. One in particular, a young girl named Laura, had taken to Amanda and been quite informative. She found herself giggling at all the dirty little details those women had shared.

"Okay, none of that," Reggie scolded. "Must share all jokes with your wingman. It's a rule."

Leaning closer to Reggie, she lowered her voice. "I now know one of the players has a foot fetish. Another one likes a little bondage action. And you know the rookie pitcher, the one they just recruited?" She paused for effect. "I hear he's watched a little too much *Bull Durham*."

"Okay, I'll bite. Meaning what?"

"Word is he's so uptight about walking in Brad's footsteps, he's resorted to wearing a garter belt under his uniform."

"Get out of here," Reggie said, eyeing the sky. "What a flipping freak."

"You haven't heard the half of it," Amanda declared, "but I'll save the rest for later."

"So which part of this are you thinking of using for your story?"

"The garter, maybe." She inspected Reggie for a reaction. "What do you think?" Not waiting for an answer, she made her case. "It fits my superstition theme and it's such good timing. You know, having written about the center fielder after Brad, doing a story about the new pitcher—"

"Is brilliant," Reggie said. "Really perfect. What about the steroids? Any tips from them?"

Amanda sighed. "No. I didn't see an opening to ask. But, the girls invited me out for a drink tomorrow night so I have another chance. It's some Saturday night deal they do every week."

Reggie's expression held surprise. "I'm impressed you got an invite."

"I hit it off with one of them. Laura's her name," Amanda said. "I think I'll work my Becker story and see if he is pulling a *Bull Durham.*"

"She's the one who's close to Tony," Reggie pointed out. "If Kevin's right about Tony, Laura could be your source. I like it. I like it a lot."

Amanda wasn't sure how she felt about the reliability of information she'd glean from the women. It was one thing to use them as sources for the men-behind-the-players theme of her column, which was based on impressions and suggestions. But it was something else entirely to use the women as sources for stories that had to be grounded in absolute fact, not speculation.

A huge order of nachos appeared on the counter. Thanks to habits formed during her years in the pool,

Amanda didn't often indulge in junk food. Given how delicious the cheese-covered chips looked, she might have to make an exception today since she was starving. As the PA sounded with the announcer reading the stats for Brad Rogers and her blood pounded, she wasn't so sure food would sate her appetite.

She was afraid it might take a big serving of Brad to ease this particular hunger.

"SAFE!"

Brad let his head fall forward as the umpire's words spilled into the air. *Son of a bitch.* His shutout record was a goner. All this pain. All this torture and the Jets had just scored, thanks to a hole in the Rays' center fielder's glove.

But it wasn't their center fielder's—or his damn peppermint oil's—fault, and Brad knew it. If only he'd had a little more heat on that last pitch…

He tried to flex his shoulder without seeming obvious, biting back another curse at the throb deep in the tissue. Forget the rest of this game, would he even make it out of this inning?

Brad watched as Coach signaled to the umpire for a time-out and headed for the mound. Looked as though the decision wasn't even his to make.

The coach stopped in front of Brad, a wad of dip puffing out his bottom lip. "You've pitched a great game, son. You pushed hard for that record and your arm is tired. We've got five on the board and their best hitter is up next. Let's give the rookie a shot to take him on. I need to see what he's got."

The muscles in Brad's gut tightened, and he ground his teeth. Not only had he lost his shot at a record, but the coach wanted to give the mound to Becker. "Simpson is 0-6 against me, Coach. Let me take him and then I'll come out."

The coach spit and then eyed Brad. "You're tired. Let Becker have him."

Brad cut his gaze from the coach, keeping it low so the camera couldn't zoom in. He wanted to argue. God, how he wanted to argue. But the truth was, he was hurting, both his body and his pride. He wasn't sure he could take another blow.

With a heavy sigh, he accepted the inevitable. "Fine. I'm out."

The crowd booed when Brad started toward the dugout, clearly unhappy with the coach's decision, and he fought the urge to ask to stay in. Brad took comfort from the fans' belief in him, even if he doubted himself.

Irritation replaced that comfort when he spotted Becker exiting the bull pen. The kid jogged toward the mound, a cocky smile on his face that seemed to say, "Don't worry, old man, I'll bring it home."

The little bastard didn't get it. Brad wanted to stalk back to the mound and tell him so. But the coach was there, ready to instruct Becker on what to expect.

Inside the dugout, Brad sat and dropped his glove to the ground. The kid wanted to be a starter. With his know it all attitude, he was lucky to be a reliever, in Brad's opinion.

He eyed the coach as he returned to the bench. "Simpson's gonna knock it out of the park, you know."

"We'll see."

"Becker gets in there and thinks he can throw a bunch of heat and strike 'em all out. He doesn't pay enough attention to batters' strengths and, worse, he ignores Kurt's signs." Brad could hear his voice rising but he was too pissed off at being replaced with the rookie to moderate it.

"I'll talk to him," Coach said. "He needs a role model."

"What he needs is an ass kicking," Brad responded.

"There are other ways of getting to him."

Brad snorted. "Short of busting him back to the minors, I don't know how."

The sound of a bat making contact with a ball drew their attention, and the coach cursed under his breath.

Simpson had just hit it out of the park.

BY THE TIME Brad entered the locker room, Amanda and several other members of the press were already there. He'd already dealt with numerous television cameras and the stupid question of the night. "How does it feel to be so close to a third shut out and miss it?"

How the hell do you think it feels? Like shit. It felt like shit. Brad had said as much, although not with that exact language. Normally, he kept his mouth shut when the camera rolled, reciting only management-approved sound bites. But not today. Not when he felt this foul.

Watching Becker take the mound with that smart-ass sneer on his pretty boy face had been pure torture. Watching Simpson smash one of the kid's fastballs out of the park had been pure satisfaction. And since the run hadn't cost the game, Brad didn't feel one bit of guilt.

As his locker came into view, he spotted Becker in deep conversation with Amanda. Brad mumbled a curse as he realized the rookie was in hard play to win the bet.

Eyeing Amanda's sultry curves displayed in the black skirt she wore, Brad ground his teeth. He'd handed over the mound to the kid. He'd be damned if he was handing over Amanda.

In fact, a good night of hot, sweaty sex would go a long way toward improving his disposition. The sooner he got Amanda's curvy little body beneath his, the better.

Brad shoved his glove into his locker, then focused on Amanda. The line of her neck was exposed as she laughed at what the rookie was saying. He imagined pressing his lips right there. Inhaling her sweet scent. Hearing her moan with the pleasure he gave her.

His competitive side flared as he watched the rookie work her. This was one battle the kid might as well give up. Brad had already decided Amanda was his.

Shoving aside his pain and fatigue, Brad started walking. Sidestepping a reporter's question, his attention was on only one thing.

He'd lost his shot at a record today. He wasn't losing this bet, too.

AMANDA KNEW the moment Brad walked into the locker room. No. She felt it. And try as she might to concentrate on the answers coming out of the rookie reliever, Casey Becker, she was thinking about Brad.

Her gaze traveled in his direction, sliding down his long, muscular frame encased in tight baseball pants. Damn, the man was hot. She'd take him dressed over other men wearing only towels any day.

Then again, she wouldn't mind Brad...undressed.

She swallowed and forced herself to focus on Casey, who appeared more interested in flirting than answering her questions. She was ready to scream. Funny how the banter and innuendo hadn't bothered her when Brad delivered it.

"I hear you're pretty superstitious about your pitching," Amanda commented. "Did luck help you recover from that home run you gave up?"

"What?" Surprise flashed across Casey's chiseled face. "Who told you that? No, I don't believe in luck. It's just me and the batter out there. No false sense of security. Brad's getting old. He needs necklaces and luck. I don't."

The Brad lashing had been unexpected. Hmm. Could someone be a bit jealous? Brad might have lost a shot at a record today, but he'd pitched a good game. Clearly, following in the star pitcher's footsteps had the rookie a bit rattled.

Amanda decided to leave the nastiness alone and redirect him back to her story. "I heard you're a fan of *Bull Durham*. The pitcher in that movie," she said, "well, he wore garters for luck."

His face reddened instantly and he threw his hands in the air, yelling out to the locker room. "Who the hell is telling everyone I wear garters for luck again? Tony!" Laughter filled the air but Tony was nowhere to be found.

"Slumming for gossip, I see."

Jack appeared by Becker's side, his voice raking Amanda's nerves.

She opened her mouth to speak, but the rookie intervened. "That's not a nice thing to say to a lady."

Jack smirked. "This isn't a lady. This is the Gossip Queen."

Amanda felt her temper building. She hated her work being called gossip, but she wasn't about to let Jack know he was getting to her.

"Yes," Amanda said to Casey. "I've already planned to expose your dirty little secrets. Tomorrow the world will know that you are from another planet and have superhuman strength brought to you by the sun. I'm also going to reveal the really naughty secret. I'm going to tell them about the how silver saps your abilities. Then you'll never throw another fastball again."

Casey chuckled. "You're funny, Amanda." He gave Jack a pointed look. "You gotta admit, she's pretty funny."

With supreme satisfaction, Amanda noted Jack's irritated expression. She might have pushed him further if Brad hadn't chosen that moment to appear.

"Jack," Brad said, giving the man a short nod, before turning his attention on Amanda. The gleam in his eyes was nothing shy of sizzling as he offered her a private greeting. "Hello." His voice was low, more friendly than when he'd addressed Jack. Even a bit intimate.

He ignored Casey altogether.

"Hi," she said. "Good pitching tonight."

"Not as good as I wanted it to be," he admitted, and quickly changed the subject. "I need to grab a shower before we do that interview. Meet you in fifteen?"

"Okay. Where?"

"Why don't you join us at Spirals for the postgame party?" Casey interjected. "Then you can interview me, too." He motioned to Jack. "Your competition will be there, won't you, Jack?"

The irritation on Jack's face deepened into a scowl. Any chance to agitate him further added incentive for her to accept the invitation. Not that she would have declined.

"That works for me," Amanda agreed, smiling at Jack before giving Casey a nod. She turned to Brad. "Does that work for you?"

Brad's gaze flickered over Casey, and for a moment, she could have sworn she saw irritation in his expression. Before she could be certain, he had his attention on her, his baby blues promising far more than an interview. "That works," he said. "I'll see you there."

His gaze lingered on her a second too long before he departed, walking away, giving her a delicious view of his stellar backside.

"I have real news to report. See you tonight," Jack said to Casey.

Amanda endured a few more minutes of the rookie's flirtation, in an effort to get the story. It didn't work. She needed more to write the article she had in mind. She'd have to work on it at the bar.

When she finally managed to ease away from him and head toward the exit, she couldn't help but wonder about the rest of the evening. What would she learn about Brad? Who was the real man behind the pitcher?

And why did the idea of finding out appeal so much?

6

BRAD LEANED against the bar, his first beer in hand, barely touched. He didn't want the damn thing, but someone had shoved it at him, so he'd accepted.

The band on stage delivered a sad country song. Cigarette smoke filled the room with a musty smell that he normally wouldn't notice, but tonight it irritated him.

It had been Tony's turn to pick the postgame spot, and he'd gone for the crowd and loud band. As always.

Truth be told, Brad had only showed up for Amanda. He'd much rather be at home, icing his arm in peace. Instead, here he was, trying to ignore his injury and angling for a way to win this bet. His mission tonight: get Amanda naked and in his bed. Any bed, for that matter.

At that moment, Becker edged into the spot beside him and ordered a beer. "What's up, old man?"

"You tell me, kid," Brad said. "You don't know how to read signs or what?" He didn't want to get into this tonight, didn't want to get distracted from Amanda, but he was too pissed off to let it go.

"What's that supposed to mean?"

"When Kurt gives you a sign, take it. That's what it means. He asked for a curveball and you threw a fastball."

"You're Kurt's messenger now? He can't talk for

himself?" Becker grunted. "And Simpson expected a curveball," he argued. "I wasn't about to give it to him."

"Apparently, he expected heat because he stroked it right out of the park," Brad countered.

"That was the only hit they got off me."

"Because you followed the signs after that."

The bartender slid Becker's glass of draft across the counter and he tossed a few bills down. "I finished what you couldn't and you don't like it."

Brad wanted to shake the kid for his stupidity. "You're making the wrong choices, Becker. You shouldn't be blowing off advice from the guys who have been around longer than you. Show some respect."

"Maybe you old guys need to show me some respect. I got the arm to put this team in the playoffs if you'd just get out of my way. Management came after me in the draft and waved a big fat contract. Rumor has it they're not offering you shit. There's *your* sign. Your days as star pitcher are over, so step aside and let the real talent in." Becker grabbed his glass and stomped away.

Brad downed his beer, suddenly grateful he'd accepted it. He'd barely had time to swallow when Jack sat on the bar stool next to him.

"Sucked to lose that record," he said.

"We won the game," Brad countered, sick of hearing about his lost record. "In the end, that's what counts."

"Tony's next," Jack said. "He's charging after that home run record." He took a drink. "Think he'll get it?"

Tony was one of the best hitters Brad had ever seen. "Hell, yes. He's got rocket fuel behind that bat."

"Some say it's more than rocket fuel."

"What's that supposed to mean?" Brad asked. A

warning bell sounded in his head. Jack had been acting differently ever since he took that new job, giving off a vibe that set Brad on edge. For whatever reason, he didn't trust the guy to write the players' side the way he used to. This suggestion that Tony was juicing reinforced Brad's caution around Jack.

"Some say Tony's rush toward the record came out of nowhere. That he got really good really fast." He paused. "Maybe too fast."

Agitated, Brad pushed off the bar, facing Jack. "I don't know where you're going with this," he said, his voice low and tight, "but I don't like it."

Tony was doing well, and someone wanted to steal that from him. Brad understood how that felt. The past year had been him trying to save what everyone wanted to take.

"Whoa there, partner," Jack said. "I'm just giving you a heads-up. It's floating around. People are talking. They're saying he's juicing."

Brad didn't believe Tony was taking steroids for a minute. "Who's your source?"

"You know I can't tell you that."

"You're the only one I hear talking, Jack." Brad leaned in close so his point would hit home. "Make sure you get your facts straight before you go shooting off your mouth."

"I'm trying to get the facts right now," Jack argued. "Talk to me. Help me get it straight."

"There's nothing to talk about. Tony works hard and it shows."

"I hope you're right." Jack's eyes narrowed. "Desperate people do desperate things."

"You're crazy, Jack."

"Maybe I am," Jack conceded. "But maybe I'm not. What if Tony wants that record so badly he's willing to risk anything to get it? What if he's fighting an injury? This is big for his career. He'd do what had to be done to hang tough. Maybe he even has encouragement. Maybe a team doc offers him a solution."

Brad understood the fear of losing your career better than anyone. Hiding an injury might not be smart, but it wasn't the same as using drugs. Tony wouldn't stoop to that.

"Sometimes players get pretty desperate to save their careers," Jack added. "I'm sure you can sympathize. Being up for contract renewal and not signing yet. Makes you wonder about that fight you had. Then there was the surgery. Maybe you don't look like such a good prospect for management."

Did Jack know he was injured again? Was that what this was about? Brad searched Jack's face for answers, but found nothing. Jack had been good to him during his fight ordeal by printing stories that showed a positive side to the entire mess. And Brad appreciated that.

"I haven't signed a new contract because I haven't decided where to sign. Don't forget, I'm already in The Show. You, on the other hand, have never quite made it there. Local paper, local news. Nothing more. Maybe you want to make The Show and you're the one getting desperate. So much so you'd hurt people who've given you their trust." Brad's accusations weren't entirely accurate since Jack was doing well for himself. But he wanted the guy to know how it felt to have his Achilles' heel pushed so he'd back off.

Jack scrubbed a hand over his jaw in obvious frustration. "I've always taken care of this team. Never once have I printed a story without getting the players' side of the issue."

"That's true. But desperate people do desperate things. Those were your words." He paused for impact. "Maybe you're the desperate one, not Tony. Maybe you're trying to make a story where one doesn't exist to snag a bit of attention."

"You're wrong," Jack insisted, his expression stormy.

"Time will tell. Either way, this conversation is over." Brad didn't wait for a reply, he just walked away.

That Jack might know about his injury bothered Brad far more than Amanda's knowing did. Why, he didn't know, and he didn't care to examine. He felt in his gut that Jack had become a problem. Yet one more thing Brad would have to keep an eye on.

The tension and frustration he felt spiked and he wished like hell Amanda would get here. He needed a healthy dose of sex-induced amnesia and she was just the woman to give it to him.

POSSIBLE HEADLINES for her feature on Casey Becker played in her head as Amanda entered the noisy bar, feeling the flutter of nerves in her stomach. She could easily blame the nerves on the need to score big with her second column, but she knew it was more than that.

She was nervous about seeing Brad again. The distinct hum of sexual excitement burned within her, all the more enticing because she couldn't allow herself to indulge. Still, she searched the crowd for him.

Reggie had offered to escort her to the bar, but Amanda had declined, thinking she could meet the team in a social situation without someone holding her hand. But these crazy sensations she had were making her second-guess her decision. With Reggie present, the situation with Brad would stay professional. Temptation couldn't be given in to.

She stood in the doorway and pondered calling Reggie. At best, he'd be a stalling tactic. She knew herself well enough to acknowledge she couldn't hide from her attraction to Brad forever. It was there. It wasn't going away anytime soon. She'd simply have to cope.

Scanning the crowd, Amanda wished she had changed clothes and freshened up. Everyone wore jeans and the women all looked groomed and gorgeous, while she still wore the same makeup and clothing she'd put on twelve hours before. Drab and dull was so not the image she wanted to project.

She stiffened her spine. Leaving wasn't an option. Establishing rapport with the team was too important. She'd seen Brad's mistrust of her regarding his arm. Hopefully the fact that she hadn't made his injury news would win confidence and help sway the team to her side. This bar was the perfect venue to let the players get to know her and trust her. A voice inside her head reminded her she'd betray that trust when she cracked the steroid-use story, but she ignored the nudge. Rapport first, digging for a story later.

Decision made, Amanda began weaving through the crowd, trying to locate the team. She sidestepped a laughing female just before connecting with her high-heeled boot. The next thing she knew, the wayward contents of someone's glass splashed in her face.

She stood there, unable to move for the sticky dampness clinging to her skin and hair. Great. Just what she needed—a layer of alcohol and soda on top of drab and dull. "This is so not my night," she mumbled, wiping liquid from her cheek.

"Damn," a familiar male voice said. "You okay?"

A drool-worthy—and dry—Brad appeared in front of her. And she resembled a drenched rat. "I'm fine," she said. "Just wet."

Brad grinned. "A man shouldn't leave a woman wet and unattended now, should he?"

She would have blushed at the innuendo, but he didn't give her a chance. "Let's get you to a bathroom," he said, grabbing her hand to pull her through the crowd.

They maneuvered through the maze of tables, chairs and people. Amanda couldn't help but notice Brad's backside looked as hot in Levi's as it did in baseball pants. Long before she'd finished her inspection, they stopped in front of the ladies' room.

"Thanks," she said, tugging to retrieve her hand from his grasp.

He held on a second longer. "I'll wait for you here."

She didn't argue. She just wanted to clean up. Inside the restroom, Amanda examined her reflection in the long expanse of mirrors and cringed.

With the help of paper towels, the brush from her purse and the hand dryer, she managed to repair her appearance in short time. Even so, she didn't want to go back out into the throng. She was done with too much noise and too many people. She would much rather be snuggled in bed watching a good movie than pretending to enjoy the bar scene.

But she needed a story. She needed to go back out there and make nice with the team. She needed to face Brad. Her stomach fluttered and she pressed her hand to her midsection. Good lord, the man got to her. One look from his baby blues and her knees were like noodles.

She couldn't let her nerves get to her. Amanda took a deep breath and shoved away from the sink, forcing herself to start walking. And as promised, Brad was waiting for her on the other side of the door. He rested one broad shoulder against the wall, arms crossed over that broad, T-shirt-clad chest.

The minute he saw her, he straightened, the corners of his lips lifting as he gave her a quick, but thorough, once-over. "You look good as new," he said.

"Thanks for the help navigating. Size makes a difference," she said, then realizing the implication of what she'd said felt her cheeks warm. Afraid her attraction to Brad was written all over her face, she lowered her lashes, trying to erase the evidence with several blinks.

Before she could refocus, before she knew what was happening, Brad pulled her close. He leaned down, his mouth next to her ear, his breath warm on her neck. "Incoming traffic," he said. "You were almost trampled again."

Being pressed so close to Brad was nothing less than explosive. In some remote corner of her mind, Amanda was aware of a large group of women squeezing past them. Remote because it was near impossible to think of anything but Brad's legs resting against hers, and the intimate touch of his hand low on her back. She wanted his hand to venture south, to cup her backside. Maybe he'd caress her thigh, encourage it to wrap around his leg so that their sexiest parts would be pressed together.

A shiver of excitement raced down her spine, and her body ached in all the right places. No, the *wrong* places, she reminded herself. Brad was off limits. Too bad the reality check did nothing to stop the awareness ripping through her body, heating her from head to toe.

Somehow, Amanda forced herself to take a step back. He resumed his position against the wall, his expression a mixture of temptation and amusement, as if he knew she was running scared. Which, of course, she was. And it was stupid. Why run?

Well, except for the fact that she had a reputation to protect—her own and that of the other female journalists who took grief for simply being women. Falling all over Brad wouldn't do much for her professionally, even if it might be enjoyable.

Anything she might have said was cut off by a female voice. "Hey, Amanda. I didn't know you were coming tonight. I'm so excited you're here."

Amanda turned to see Laura, the pretty blond groupie who could be no older than twenty-two or twenty-three. She greeted Brad, then said to Amanda, "Wait for me. I have a table with a bunch of the guys. You can join us."

This was a perfect escape, actually. Amanda could use a minute away from Brad to cool off a little. "Sounds good."

"Excellent," Laura said. "Back in a second."

"Hanging with the groupies now?" Brad inquired.

A defensive response slipped out. "You do. Why not me?"

"I don't," Brad said.

"That's not how I hear it."

"It was a long time ago."

"And now you're above all that?" She leaned on the wall, mimicking his posture.

"Now I'm at a different place in my life and my career."

"Which is where?" she asked.

Laura exited the ladies' room before Amanda could get Brad's answer—an answer she'd really wanted to hear. "I'm back," Laura said, stating the obvious. "The line was too long to wait."

"Well," Amanda said to Brad. "I guess I'll go grab a drink."

Brad eyed Laura a moment, then motioned for her to give them a minute.

"Oh," Laura said. "I'll wait right over there." She pointed to a corner bar.

So much for escaping. The minute Laura was out of hearing distance, Brad said, "I guess you're not ready yet."

Ready? For him?

"Ready?" Amanda asked, her voice not quite as firm as she'd hoped.

"For the interview," he said, a half smile giving him a sexy dimple in his right cheek. "Let me know when you're ready."

She felt her cheeks warm. "Oh. Yes. The interview." Not sex. *The interview.* The one she hadn't asked for but he'd offered to give. The one she couldn't begin to think about while she could still feel his nice, hard chest beneath her palms. "Give me a couple minutes to say hi to everyone and I'll be…ready."

"I'm looking forward to it."

LATER AMANDA SAT in a booth next to Laura, with Tony on the other side of the young groupie. Laura clung to him like a second skin, obviously smitten with the ballplayer. Tony, on the other hand, seemed more interested in the brunette fawning over the team catcher, Kurt Caverns.

Kurt, who could deliver a joke with a straight face and dry tone better than anyone she'd ever met, appeared more attached to his cowboy hat than the brunette.

Amanda listened to Laura praise Tony's amazing bat and experienced a touch of empathy for the girl. Laura was headed toward heartache. Her adoration of Tony was obvious in her words and gestures. And in the way she seemed to overlook that he didn't return her affection.

Kelli's God complex rules came to Amanda. Athletes were players. Safe for a good time, but never ever safe for the involvement of the heart. Maybe she should share that little tidbit with Laura. Maybe she could give Laura perspective, help her realize there were other men who would appreciate and respect her.

Right. Amanda was in no position to be giving advice about perspective. She was having a hard enough time keeping Brad out of her thoughts right now.

With a sigh, Amanda reached for her margarita, and took a drink, trying to escape Brad's presence. No, she couldn't see him, but she could sense him, as sure as she could still smell the spicy cologne he wore. The scent lingered on her clothes from when he'd pulled her close. The heat of his body still surrounded her, warmed her. Even though logic told her he'd be trouble, her libido teased her with images of how good he'd be between the sheets. She was aching to remember what a good time felt like.

Lord, she was in deep trouble. Brad Rogers had gotten to her. The fact that she was a big ball of sexual need wasn't helping one bit. Who knew avoiding the pleasures of male companionship would make her so vulnerable to lust?

And as much as she wanted that interview with Brad,

Amanda knew she had to exercise caution. She was far from control when in his company and it seemed only a matter of time before logic abandoned her to lust.

At that moment, Jack disrupted her thoughts by sliding into the booth next to the brunette. His sports coat had been replaced by a western shirt. "Dug up any gossip yet?" he asked Amanda.

"She didn't have to dig," Kurt said, his manner friendly, as if he liked Jack and was teasing him. "I've been telling her all kinds of shit about you."

"I hope you haven't gotten to all the good stuff," Jack said, contempt in his expression, despite his easy tone. "I might have something to add."

Before Amanda could reply, Casey appeared at the table, his attention on her. Blond, blue-eyed and well-dressed, he was a catch. But he was a kid to Amanda. A cocky one at that.

"Would you like to dance, Amanda?" he asked, clearly broadcasting his interest.

Jack snorted and crossed his arms in front of his chest. "Oh, please."

"What's wrong? Upset because he didn't ask you?" Amanda taunted.

Tony let out a bark of laughter. "That would be a sight."

"Shaking your ass won't get you readers," Jack snapped.

"But it will get her a story," Laura chimed in.

Okay, Amanda didn't need that comment. Nothing brilliant came to mind, so she went with what did. "You're an ass, Jack."

"And you, Amanda, are a wannabe who won't. You are going nowhere fast."

The words were a slap. More than once her ex had

used the exact same words. She was not a wannabe and she was not going to fail. But that didn't mean she wanted to deal with Jack's animosity anymore. Though dealing with the rookie's advances didn't hold much more appeal, at least Casey represented a possible story.

"Yes, I am," she said. "I'm going to the dance floor where I get an exclusive interview." Pushing to her feet, she faced the rookie. "Let's dance."

A few minutes later, Amanda was being twirled and maneuvered in tune with a George Strait song. Not only was the movement murder on her toes, but it also rendered talking impossible. So much for that exclusive interview. At this rate, her night was headed for a total bust.

SHOVING CASH into the hands of the band's manager, Brad ensured the next song would be a slow one. Adrenaline pulsed through him as he headed for the dance floor, prepared to take control of the situation, just as he did on the baseball field. Becker had had more than his share of Amanda while Brad had not had near enough.

Arriving at the edge of the dance floor, he scanned the couples and zeroed in on his target. Anticipating the change in music, he weaved his way to where Becker showed off his two-step skills. Brad stopped slightly behind Amanda, surprised at the rush of possessiveness the sight of Becker's hand on her waist stirred in him. Surprised, too, at how much he wanted to pull Amanda close. How much he wanted Amanda, period. Bet or no bet, Amanda would be his and Becker would be gone.

Oh, yeah, Becker was about to get a lesson he wouldn't soon forget.

7

"I BELIEVE THIS is my dance."

Amanda glanced to her right to find Brad standing by her side, his gaze fixed on her.

"Forget it," Becker said. "You can head back to your seat and wallow in your beer."

Brad didn't even look at Becker. He focused on her, sending a silent message that spoke volumes. He wanted a whole lot more than this dance. "I believe that's up to Amanda," he said.

The moment built as they all stood their ground. Around them, people danced, while the three of them remained still. Despite what she told herself, she knew Brad was asking for more than a dance or another feature in her column. This was a turning point. Whatever decision she made now would dictate whether logic or lust ruled. If she said no, she sensed that Brad might never again pursue her. If she said yes…

Who was she kidding? The decision had been made the second he'd adjusted his towel that first day. She turned to Casey. "Brad owes me an interview."

Casey stared at her, disbelief and agitation on his face. He didn't let go. In fact, his grip tightened, became possessive.

Amanda had the distinct feeling his desire to hold on had nothing to do with her and everything to do with Brad. The overload of testosterone flying between the two men had her thinking there would be trouble. She wanted no part of whatever pissing contest these two were engaged in, and was about to say so when Casey eased his hold, then stepped away.

"Don't think this is over," he said. But she wasn't sure to whom he directed the warning.

The song ended, and without hesitation, Brad pulled her close. With a smooth step, he rotated, giving Casey his back.

Brad's hand settled on her lower back as a slow melody by Garth Brooks began. Almost as if he knew it would. Something was up.

Even as distracted as she was by his sexy scent that was so much more enticing with proximity, she wasn't letting him off the hook. "You knew the song was going to change."

He didn't even try to deny her claim. "Not only did I know it, I made sure of it."

She studied him. "You like making him mad, don't you?"

"Yeah," he admitted. His eyes darkened, warmed. "But that has nothing to do with why I wanted a slow song."

"Brad—"

He touched his finger to her lips, shutting down her objection. "It's just a dance."

They could claim this was *just a dance,* but they both knew more than that was happening between them. Every second they spent together was fuel on a simmering flame.

Slowly, Brad eased his finger away from her mouth, caressing her cheek as he did. She swallowed hard, her

throat suddenly dry, the heaviness of arousal building
in her limbs. That heaviness grew as Brad took a subtle
step forward, dissolving the distance between them.
Their thighs brushed, not so close that they'd draw attention but close enough to inspire all kinds of sensual
images in Amanda's mind.

This couldn't happen here for the team and Jack to
see. She needed to delay this seduction until a more ap-
propriate time. In a desperate attempt to regain her com-
posure, Amanda started talking. "What's the story with
you and the rookie?"

"I could ask you the same thing. The kid seems to
like you, Amanda."

"You're avoiding the question."

They'd danced their way to a corner away from the
speakers and the music wasn't as loud. He bent down,
his face close to hers. "I couldn't hear you."

She wasn't sure she believed that. But on the off
chance he hadn't heard her question, she stood on her
tiptoes to repeat it near to his ear.

One of his hands splayed across her back, inching
her closer, and suddenly Amanda couldn't remember
what she'd wanted to say. "Behave, Brad."

As she started to ease away from him, he stopped her,
his mouth lingering mere inches from hers. Their eyes
locked in a stare that almost knocked the breath out of
her. For several seconds, she lost herself in Brad. In
what her body was feeling, desiring.

"Behaving is overrated," he finally responded.

Was it ever.

Someone bumped into them and jolted Amanda to
her senses. Could the others see them here in the
shadows? Did it look as though they were doing some-

thing inappropriate? Her gaze slid around the room, and she was thankful to find they were hidden in this crowded corner.

She shoved away from Brad, forceful enough to send him a message this time, but not enough to draw attention. She didn't know what to say to him, didn't know how to express the emotions colliding inside her, so she started walking.

Damn, how had she let the situation get so out of hand? She fumed. Yes, she'd been a willing participant. And while she may not have encouraged that little corner interlude, she hadn't stopped it. What had Brad been thinking putting on that seduction display for all to see? A club filled with reporters and ball players was not the place for them to explore the thing going on between them.

A hand on her arm stopped her and she turned to face Brad. "Don't go. Let me buy you a drink." The music changed again and people began to two-step around them. "Please."

The entreaty got to her. "Fine," she said, tugging her arm free. "But I want a real interview. And don't try any more cute moves."

He nodded and waved her forward, obviously having no trouble hearing her now. She headed toward the bar, wishing she had skipped this night out.

There would be plenty of time to get to know the team, but *no,* she'd had to do it now. Her drive to over-achieve had spurred the competitive need to defeat Jack, so she'd pushed herself rather than letting the relationships evolve. Instead of playing flirtatious games with the team's star pitcher, she could be at the hotel working on making her next feature better than the first ones.

Sure, she wanted another interview with Brad, and she wanted a bit more from Casey for her next piece. But she had tomorrow and Monday in the locker room with them. And if they didn't deliver either of those days, she had outlined several other good story ideas that she could make great.

It was time to cut her losses tonight. She'd get out of here before she did any damage to her career. And once she'd calmed down, she would figure out a plan to deal with Brad and her hard-to-control desire for him.

"I need to leave," she announced as she faced him. "I'm not ready to interview and this isn't the place for it."

He bent at the knees, bringing himself to eye level with her. "The back room is quieter."

"I'm leaving," she said firmly.

"I'll walk you to your car." Brad wasn't giving up easily.

"No." She needed to get away from Brad to clear her head. "I'm fine. I'm going to say good night to everyone."

"I'll meet you at the door."

"No," she said again, but it was too late. He was already headed to the bar, removing his wallet as if to pay a tab. Fine, she'd deal with him outside.

Ten minutes later, Amanda had said her goodbyes. She wasn't surprised to see Tony dancing with the brunette he'd been flirting with, nor was she surprised to see Laura sitting at the table looking dejected. Jack hovered over her. Amanda suspected that any sympathy from Jack came with an agenda. She thought about intervening on Laura's behalf, but she didn't know the actual situation, so her efforts could worsen the circumstances. Besides, she had her own mess to worry about.

Somehow, she'd invited the very man she was trying

to escape, the one who made her so hot he might as well have *sex* as a middle name, to join her in a dark parking lot.

Brilliant. Just brilliant.

She'd have to get rid of him quickly so she could find peace in her hotel room. Simple. She'd wish him a quick adios and be on her way.

But her bravado disappeared in the parking lot when Brad was nowhere in sight. In fact, the relief she should have experienced knowing she'd avoided another encounter with Mr. Temptation was not to be found. Instead, a solid ball of disappointment settled deep in her gut, refusing to be dismissed.

With a sigh, she walked to her car. The exterior of the club was surprisingly deserted. The music from the band blasted noise into the night and then became muffled by the door shutting behind her.

"Amanda."

Brad's voice sounded from her left, startling her.

"Will you stop doing that!" she snapped.

"Stop what?"

Being so damn irresistible. Out loud, she said, "Stop sneaking up on me."

He gave her a sexy, lopsided grin. "I'll do my best." He stepped forward, closing in on her.

Amanda angled her chin upward to see his face. "Aren't you taller than most pitchers?"

"I am."

"How tall?" she asked, going into her safe zone, her interview mode.

"Six-three."

Interesting. "Is it hard to pitch to shorter players? I mean, how does height impact your play?"

"Uh-huh. We aren't doing the interview in the parking lot," he said. "Where's your car?"

"At the side of the building."

"Mine, too," he said, pulling his keys from his pocket.

"You're leaving?"

"Actually," he said, "I thought we might conduct the interview at a coffee shop down the road."

She wasn't really surprised by his suggesting a more intimate setting. What did surprise her was his facade of innocence. As if they were really talking about an interview.

"I don't think that's a good idea," she said, shoving her purse up her shoulder and crossing her arms.

He held his hands out like an offering of sorts. His muscular forearms grabbed her gaze for some reason. They were strong. Sexy. She forced her attention to his face.

"It's just coffee and the offer of a one-on-one interview," he said.

When she didn't immediately answer, he added, "The coffee shop is only two blocks away. It's a busy place. As in lots of people besides you and me."

"I want a real interview. No holding back." If she was going to put herself in the line of more temptation, she wanted it to be for a justifiable reason.

"And you'll get it," he assured her quickly.

"Why should I believe that?" she asked, not sold yet. "You didn't even answer my question a minute ago about pitching to shorter batters."

"We're in a parking lot."

"Reporters corner you in all kinds of crazy places."

A smile hinted on his lips. "You're one tough

cookie." He rested his weight on his back foot and seemed to consider a minute. "I'll give you a lead-in now." He touched his necklace. "You were right. I hate taking it off. It does feel lucky."

"Old news. I knew that, even if you didn't admit it."

"Okay, then. It was my father's. He played for U.T. when he was in college, too, and he was my biggest fan, aside from my mom."

"*Was* your biggest fan?" Amanda asked. "Where is he now?"

He hesitated, then his voice softened. "He died before I made it to U.T., let alone the pros."

Stunned by his admission, Amanda blinked. "I'm sorry. I feel like a complete idiot for that last question."

"It's okay. I'd prefer you not print that."

"I won't print anything you tell me not to." She did want him to trust her. She wanted all the players to trust her, but Brad more so than anyone.

"Fair enough," he said. "So…yes to coffee?"

Torn, Amanda contemplated his offer. She wanted this interview, yet agreeing to it now went against her plan to put space between them until she had a strategy for dealing with him. It took her to a one-on-one setting with Brad when she wasn't quite equipped for the potential intimacy.

Finally the lure of the interview and a great feature won the battle. "Fine. I'll follow you."

Satisfaction flared in Brad's eyes, though his tone was unaffected. Monotone, even. "That works."

Amanda pointed to her sad rental car. "This is me. The rental place didn't take very good care of me."

"I see that." He eyed the car then indicated a black pickup. "That's me."

She couldn't contain her surprise. "You drive that?"

He lifted one eyebrow. "You expected something else?"

"Ah, yeah. A Corvette. A Porsche. A typical jock kind of car. You left those at home tonight, I guess?"

"I outgrew the obsession with fancy cars several years ago," he said, "About the time I outgrew groupies, by the way."

"Point taken," she said, recognizing the warning not to make assumptions about him.

"I do admit to owning a '69 Mustang that is as sweet as they come."

"Really?" she asked. "Funny. My dad does, too. Actually, he's got a 1963 coupe and a 1967 turbo."

"Sweet," he said. "I'd love to get a look at those babies. Did he restore them?"

"Oh, yes. They were his pet projects." Amanda didn't know why she was telling him this. Her personal stuff was just that…personal. She motioned toward her car. "I'll follow you."

He hesitated a moment, as if reconsidering what he was going to say. "All right, then."

Amanda got in and turned the ignition. The car didn't start. In fact, it didn't make a sound at all. She tried again. And again.

Her head dropped to the steering wheel. "I don't believe this." She must be setting some kind of record for most random acts of misfortune tonight.

A knock sounded on the window. Like the cowboy who wears the white hat, Brad had come to her rescue. As much as she appreciated his presence, she hated that circumstances were conspiring to make her appear as though she needed rescuing.

He pulled open the door and she could have sworn

he smiled. But then the smile was gone, replaced with concern. Good thing. She might have hurt him if he gloated at a time like this.

"Ride with me," Brad offered. "You can call the rental company on the way to the coffee shop."

"I need to wait on a new car."

"Tell them to deliver it to wherever you're staying. I'll drop you there after the interview."

That sounded logical. Except for the part that landed Brad at her hotel. That sounded so good. Too good.

She got out of the car. Brad was facing her, his hand on the door so that his broad shoulders enclosed her. She could almost feel the warmth of his body. She remembered how it felt when he held her, and the memory teased her with possibilities. With her own wants and desires.

Call a cab, a voice inside her head said. She ignored the voice. "Okay. Let's go."

She wanted Brad Rogers. But before she could allow herself to have him she had to think through the implications and be prepared for the consequences.

She would always have to face Brad the next day. At the games. In the locker room. On the bus or plane while traveling.

And someone would find out. They always did in these situations. It was impossible to keep sex hidden, especially in these kinds of circumstances, with players and reporters being so close. For Brad, sleeping with the new reporter would be a notch on his bedpost. It might even make him a hero to the other guys. For Amanda, it would damage her reputation and her career. There would always be doubt and innuendo about how far she'd go to get a story. Was she prepared for that?

It was a high price to pay. With any other man she

would have walked away without a qualm. But her sexual infatuation with Brad was too strong to be ignored. So she had to figure out a way to do the man until he was out of her system while protecting her job.

Easy. Not.

8

BRAD PULLED HIS TRUCK into a spot in a far corner of the hotel parking lot, unable to find a spot closer to Amanda's room. Apparently, there was a convention here and the place was packed.

The rental agency had told Amanda she'd have a new vehicle delivered to her hotel in one to four hours, which made their coffee date impossible. He had mixed feelings about that.

On the one hand, a little coffee and conversation would have eased Amanda's obvious apprehension about being alone with him. Certainly it would have cooled the heat between them a degree or two, so that sex wasn't such a big deal.

On the other hand, he wanted her so much, he didn't want to ease the tension between them. He wanted her hot and breathless and as wrapped up in him as he was in her. Already he was fascinated by little quirky traits about her, such as the way she rambled and became jumpy when she was nervous. He'd never known a woman who made him think about sex and sin so much, yet still managed to be adorable and sweet.

The *adorable and sweet* part made him nervous because it usually signaled relationship and commitment. He wasn't ready for that. A little under-the-covers action was one thing. He had too much on the line right now for anything more. He'd seen guys get distracted by women. Seen their play suffer for it, too. Until he had a signed contract in hand, there would be no distractions.

So as long as Amanda accepted that there would only be sex between them, he was good to go.

"I'll walk you to the door," he said, killing the ignition. Darkness engulfed the cab of the truck.

"It's okay," Amanda said. "Thanks for the ride."

"Rain check on coffee?"

She smiled. "Rain check on an interview?"

"We can still do the interview," he said, not ready for this night to end. "What do you want to know?"

"A little while ago you didn't want to interview in a parking lot."

"I guess I changed my mind."

"I can't interview you now," she said. "Not in a pitch-dark truck."

He twisted in his seat to face her. The space between them begged to be eliminated. All he had to do was slide forward and reach for her. "You could invite me in."

"I'm not going to do that, and you know it."

"Yeah," he said. His current position put pressure on his arm and he flexed his fingers before he could stop himself. "I know."

Her gaze went to his arm then lifted to his face, the poor lighting making her expression impossible to read.

"I was a swimmer headed to the Olympics," she said. "I wanted it more than I wanted my next breath. It…was everything to me."

"What happened?" he asked, his voice low, his gut clenched with the pain in her voice. That pain hit close to home. It landed on his fear about his arm, about losing his dream. His *life*. Ball was all he knew.

She stared down at the seat. Her response came slowly. "A knee injury is what happened. I tried to hide it. Actually, I did hide it. Even from my dad."

"He's a doctor, you said?"

She nodded. "With the NFL. My knee had been a problem everyone thought I'd beat."

"But you hadn't," he said, knowing exactly what she had gone through.

"No. It flared up right before qualification rounds, which just happened to be smack in the middle of football season."

"So your father was distracted."

"Not as much as you would think, but it made avoidance a bit easier."

He let her remain silent for a while before he prodded, "What happened, Amanda?"

Biting her bottom lip, she cut her hand through the air dismissively. "The details aren't important." She fixed her attention on him. "I know what you're battling and your secret is safe with me. But that's not why I'm telling you this. I swam injured, Brad. I wasn't willing to miss my chance to qualify. And that decision cost me my dream. Don't do the same thing."

The absolute accuracy of her words took him aback. Nobody knew what he was going through. Nobody had a clue about the dilemma he was in. But Amanda did. He didn't know what to say.

When he didn't immediately reply, she made a soft, frustrated sound and reached for the door. "I don't know why I bothered to tell you all of that. Good night, Brad. Thanks for the ride."

He realized then she thought his silence meant he didn't care about the secret she'd shared. But that wasn't it. Far from it. Her willingness to open up, to caution him, made him want her more.

"Don't go," he said, stopping her departure with both words and actions. He reached for her, put his arms around her.

But when he would have pulled her close, her fists balled on his chest, preventing him. Their eyes locked, heat darting between them, a mixture of attraction and her obvious anger. "I need to go."

"Don't go," he whispered.

Several seconds passed, the warmth of her stare spreading over his body. The air crackled with passion, with attraction.

His gaze settled on her full lips, and he burned to taste her. "I really don't want you to go." He waited for a sign to take what he wanted.

Slowly, she melted into him. Brad reveled in the feel of her soft curves against his body. Her fists opened, fingers spreading, moving to his shoulders, tugging him closer.

Finally, they were kissing. Wildly, passionately. Her arms twined around his neck. Her scent was intoxicating, addictive. She tasted like cinnamon and sugar, delicious, sweet. The flavor urged him to take more, to deepen the kiss.

He stroked his tongue along hers, exploring, absorbing, teasing. This woman did crazy things to him. Made him wild. Set him on fire. The way she moaned into his mouth, slid her tongue against his, matched him stroke for stroke, told him that she wanted him as much as he did her.

He wanted all this woman was and ever could be.

That want spurred him. A primal yearning to possess her took hold. He let go of where he was, focused only on what he wanted, on what he needed.

With a quick maneuver, he had her reclined on the seat, and positioned himself on top of her. He nudged her knees apart so he could fit his rock-hard erection into the V of her body. Still kissing her, he skimmed his hand down her leg, then around to cup her sweet round ass as he pulled her tight against his hips.

He moaned as she arched into him, her hands in his hair, on his face, on his shoulders. Her leg curled over the top of his calf and she lifted herself to full contact with his erection. The sensation clenched his gut and had him thrusting to meet her. It would be so easy to shove her panties aside and bury himself deep inside her. To claim that wet heat he knew would be oh, so good.

Nearby a door slammed. Voices sounded. Laughter. Amanda froze. It was her stillness that brought Brad back to reality. He'd been too lost in Amanda to do more than remotely register the noise.

Raising his head a bit, he surveyed the lot outside the window. A group of people had parked beside them and were now unloading their baggage. "They're right next to us," he told her. "Stay down."

"Oh, no," she mumbled, and then again, more panicked. "Oh, no. Can they see us? Tell me they can't see us."

Propped up on an elbow, his erection still planted in the V of her body, he stared at her. Even in the dark, he could see the cute crinkle between her eyebrows. An urge to kiss that worry away came over him but he held back, thinking it would be inappropriate.

"It's okay," he said, reaching to brush a strand of hair from her cheek. "Stay where you are and we'll be fine."

She nodded, the crinkle deepening. He caved and bent down to kiss it.

The voices began to fade, the danger passing. "Stop worrying. They're leaving." He laughed then, the craziness of the situation becoming quite clear. "I haven't gotten busted for making out in a car since high school."

Amanda shoved at his chest. "Don't you dare laugh. There is nothing remotely humorous about this. Let me up."

"No."

"*What?*"

"No," he said, enjoying her outrage. "I'm not letting you up until you admit this is pretty funny."

"I'll admit no such thing. Let me up before they come back."

"They're not coming back." Besides, he didn't want to set her free without an invitation to her room.

"Brad!"

The level of frustration in her voice put an end to the game. "Oh, all right."

Shifting to a sitting position, he did his best to avoid the discomfort of his zipper digging in. Beside him, Amanda straightened the clothes he wanted to strip off her.

But the odds of that happening were slim. She'd shut off the fire and brought on the ice.

"I'll walk you to your door."

"I don't need to be walked." She declined even faster than the last time.

She got out of the truck and slammed the door. Brad met her at the tailgate. "A gentleman always sees a girl to the door."

"Right. *Gentleman.* We raced past that a few minutes ago, don't you think?"

Ordinarily, he would shoot back a cocky comment. One that would remind her he hadn't been alone in the front seat. But for some reason, he couldn't.

"That wasn't planned. It just happened." He wanted to reach for her, but her body language screamed at him to keep his distance. "But I'm not sorry, either, Amanda."

She pinned him in a hard stare. "This…thing, this…whatever it is between us, can't happen, is not going to happen this way. Not in some semipublic place where anyone could see. I have a job and a reputation."

"Look, I'll be more careful. And I won't tell anyone," he said, knowing he'd just forfeited the bet with the rookie but not caring. Before, it had mattered. Now it didn't. "Why would I make you look bad? You know about my arm. You could slaughter me."

Color rushed to her cheeks. "Oh, my God." The words were ground out from between clenched teeth. "You did this to hold it over my head, didn't you?"

She stalked toward the hotel. He planted himself in her path. "No," he said, realizing his mistake too late. "It's not like that. This isn't some trick to keep you from writing about my arm." She studied him, anger evident into her expression. "Amanda. I want you. That's not something a man fakes. Come on," he said. "You felt how much I want you. I know you did." Her cheeks flushed. "Think of this as a free ticket. You don't have to worry I'll tell our secret. I don't have to worry you'll tell mine. That's not such a bad thing, now is it?"

Slowly, her posture relaxed. "I don't know what to think. All I know is this was a mistake. I have to go."

Defeated, Brad let her pass, not sure why doing so bothered him so much.

"Good night, Brad," she said, her voice cutting him like a knife with its steel coldness. She walked away, ending a night that could have been filled with satisfaction, with frustration instead.

Brad didn't follow. He stood there, watching. Knowing she was right. Behaving like hormonal kids was a mistake. Their careers demanded they be smarter and more discreet than getting naked in the front of his truck.

The sexy sway of her hips was a sultry seduction, teasing him with what he couldn't have. Still, he didn't move, waiting for her to enter that building and take away the hope she'd change her mind.

Then she paused. Only a foot from the sliding glass doors, she hesitated. She faced him and, even from a distance, he saw the invitation.

9

AMANDA WATCHED Brad approach, the sexy swagger of his walk warming her the way his kiss had. Okay. Not as much as his kiss, but almost. She could still feel those muscular legs pressed between hers as they had been in his truck. His hard body fitted above hers.

Taking a deep breath, Amanda tried to calm her racing heart. She shouldn't be doing this right now. She really should be figuring out the safest way to have Brad without compromising her career. But after that make-out party there was only one option as far as Amanda could tell. Cave in to the lust and get it out of their systems. And what could be more anonymous than a room in a large hotel? As Brad had said, they both had reason to stay quiet.

With that thought, Brad stopped in front of her. His heady male scent attacked her senses with a vengeance. Oh, how she wanted him. She could feel her skin tingling. Her body craved Brad. Craved another touch, another taste.

Their eyes locked and she felt full-body contact. Her nipples tightened, the pull of arousal pulsed deep in her core.

"I reconsidered," she said, silently daring him to challenge the excuse she was about to deliver. She wished she was brave enough to skip the excuse, but she needed the pretense of work to walk through that hotel door with him by her side. "I want that interview."

Amanda waited for his response, almost wanting him to say something to screw this up. To give her a reason to back out, to behave like her usual good-girl self.

Brad studied her a long moment, his expression indiscernible. "All right, then," he said. "An interview it is."

Though his words were innocent enough, those baby blues of his blazed a degree hotter. The smoldering look he fixed on her had nothing to do with work and everything to do with them steaming up the windows of his truck.

She swallowed, not bothering with a response, deciding they needed privacy more than chatting. They walked through the lobby, his presence beside her like a soft caress across her skin. She could stop here and actually do an interview in any of the empty chairs they passed. That idea filled her with disappointment so she didn't stop. There was nothing to hold her back from the ultimate sexual encounter but herself.

At the elevator, she pushed the button, feeling more confident about her decision with each passing second. She could feel the weight of his stare, scorching her like the summer sun. Willing her to make eye contact. As if he wanted some sort of confirmation they were on the same page. Well, he'd just have to wait to find out.

The elevator opened and she stepped forward, Brad on her heels as she entered the empty car. The doors shut them inside and the air crackled with electricity. Amanda barely managed to punch the third floor button before she found herself in Brad's arms, palms pressed to rock hard muscle. She started to melt, a shiver of excitement racing down her spine.

"Just so we're clear," he said, his voice low, laced with a raspy quality that suggested arousal. "If I have you alone in a hotel room, I won't be keeping my hands to myself."

Her fingers flexed, absorbing the delicious feel of him. "I'd be disappointed if you did."

She spoke the words boldly. They were absolutely clear. His eyes darkened, and he shifted her hips to align with his. Amanda thrilled at his reaction. She thoroughly enjoyed the power to entice him.

The elevator dinged and she smiled. "Game time," she whispered as she pushed away from him.

She led him to her room, keeping her gaze averted, never giving him a chance to figure out what her idea of the *game* might be.

A swipe of the key card and she was in the room, tossing her purse in the corner, and putting distance between herself and Brad. For once, she was taking the lead position in a sexual encounter. Her past had included far too much vanilla sex. Tonight, she wanted spicy hot.

Reveling in the freedom evoked by her thoughts, she faced Brad. Moonlight spilled through the open curtains on the floor-to-ceiling windows, casting the room in a dim, sensual glow.

Brad flipped the dead bolt into place before latching the chain. Somehow, the act screamed of dominance and control. Control she wasn't willing to let him have. Not this time.

He leaned against the wall, one booted leg over the other, one hand in his pocket. The laid-back stance might have been convincing if not for the predatory gleam in his eyes. He watched, waited.

Sliding out of her jacket, she threw it onto the chair in the corner, knowing the message she was sending. Knowing her discarded clothing confirmed his expectation of what would come next.

"Nothing leaves this room," she said, cautious as always. Her inner vixen might be out to play, but the good girl had a few conditions.

He nodded. "What happens here stays here."

Her fingers went to her blouse, attracting his gaze. The mood shifted with her action, crackling with anticipation. One by one, she released the buttons, the more skin she showed, the more the air seemed to thicken, the harder it was to breathe.

Brad didn't move, didn't openly react. Yet, she could feel his hunger, his desire, a tiger ready to pounce. That pleased Amanda, encouraged her to test her seduction skills.

She shrugged out of the blouse, displaying her sheer, pink bra. She could feel his stare on her breasts like an intimate touch, and her nipples tightened into hard peaks. Never before had Amanda found herself so aroused by the look in a man's eyes.

Excitement coursed through her body. She reached for her skirt, letting it fall to the floor.

Wearing only a thong, high heels and her barely-there bra, Amanda struck a sexy pose. One hip out, hands on waist, she confronted him.

He ravished her with his eyes, and she sensed that he was on edge, ready for her. And she liked it.

Slowly, she walked toward him, closing the distance between them, watching him watch her. With each step her body pulsed, anticipated the moment he'd put those big hands on her.

She didn't stop until only a few inches separated them. His gaze flickered to her breasts. "You're beautiful, Amanda," he said, raising his eyes to hers.

The way he'd said the words, laced with arousal and desire, nearly did her in. Spurred her to speed things up, to push for satisfaction, for more Brad.

"And you," she purred, "are wearing far too many clothes." She crossed her arms, framing her breasts. "Take them off."

BRAD FOUND this bossy side of Amanda beyond sexy. If Amanda wanted him naked, he'd damn well get naked.

He tugged his shirt off, throwing it aside. But when he reached for his jeans, her hand covered his. "Not yet," she ordered.

Slowly, he eased his hands to his sides. "Good," she said. "Keep them there until I say otherwise."

That was a difficult request when the urge to take what he'd wanted since the first moment he'd met her was like rocket fuel shooting through his veins.

Her hands, soft and warm, settled at his waist. For a moment, he shut his eyes and absorbed the feel of her hands on his skin. Brad could barely breathe as she began to explore, tracing the lines of his body, teasing him with sensation after sensation. The simplest of acts became incredibly erotic.

She shifted and her legs touched his. That damn flower scent stirred his hunger while it tested his willpower. He tilted his head, letting the soft strands of her hair tickle his chin and cheek.

The scrape of her teeth on his nipple, a sharp dart of

pleasure, set him into action. He reached for her, filling his hands with that lush, round ass and molding her hips against his erection. He left no doubt how hot and hard he was for her.

Her hands gripped his biceps. Defiance flashed in her eyes. "I told you no touching."

"A man only has so much willpower, sweetheart," he drawled. He didn't give her time to argue, just claimed her mouth in a kiss that held nothing back. His tongue swept into her mouth, taking what he wanted, what he craved.

For several seconds, she held herself stiff, as if she would resist. The need to demand her submission drove him to deepen the kiss. One of her arms slid around his neck, while her hand framed his face. Her body formed to his like a soft blanket of sensual heat covering him.

Just when he thought he'd won, she surprised him. Suddenly, Amanda met his passion with a fiery response, her tongue battling his for supremacy, for the ultimate control. Stroke for stroke, demanding, taking, turning his victory into a wicked battle for dominance. And damn, the battle tasted good. Like honey mixed with cinnamon, the sweetness of her blended with the spicy woman who'd come out to play.

He swept his hand downward and, shoving aside the thin strip of her thong, trailed his fingers in her most intimate places. A sexy little sound erupted from her as she tore her mouth from his.

She stared at him, lips slightly parted and swollen from his kiss. Her fingers went to his waistband. "You are not listening. No touching unless I say so."

Tugging him forward, she angled him toward the

bed. He didn't fight her. A second later, she pushed him down to the mattress.

Immediately, she was there, too, straddling him, that lush backside settling on his erection. He moaned, desire tearing through him. Amanda smiled in response, a spark of pure mischief flashing in her eyes.

She reached around, unhooked her bra, and tossed it aside. One look at her bare breasts, and he was ready to come unglued. Screw the hands-off rule. He wanted to touch her and he intended to. But before he could make his move, Amanda arched her back, and planted her hands on his thighs behind her. With her rosy red nipples thrust in the air, she swiveled her hips against his cock, her breasts bouncing with the action.

Hungrily he took in the sensual sight she made. Primal need drove him to take more. He sat up, one arm sliding behind her back, anchoring her against his chest. His other hand covered her breast, fingers teasing the erect nipple. For several seconds they sat that way, bodies intimately connected, the mood simmering, becoming more intense.

"Why don't you want me to touch you?" he demanded, his thumb stroking her nipple. His cock jerked at the sexy sigh she gave. "You know you want me to." His lips lingered near hers, their breath mingled. "You like when I touch you, don't you?"

"I do the touching," she whispered, but she shivered as he gently tugged on the erect tip, her hips arching into him ever so slightly, as if she tried to stop herself but couldn't.

He reveled in the knowledge her resistance was fading. "That's not what I asked." His lips brushed hers before sliding along her cheek, her neck, her shoulder.

Such soft skin she had. "I asked if you like my touch," he said, his tongue lapping at her nipple and he blew on it. She shivered and whimpered.

"Tell me what you want." He blew on the stiff peak again. "Tell me."

She hid her breast with her hand, dislodging his. Brad wanted to roar with frustration. He covered her fingers with his hand, forcing her to caress herself with every shift of his own fingers and he rocked his body against hers, reminding her of the pleasure he had to give. "You'd rather do it yourself than tell me what you want?"

He pinned her with his stare. "Is that right, Amanda?"

Her lashes fluttered before she buried her face in his neck. One second. Two. Her body relaxed into his, edging them closer and more susceptible to the intense emotions spinning around them. Her hand moved, allowing him direct contact with her breast again. Then she guided his fingers with her own, telling him without words what she wanted.

Victory roared inside him, coursing through his veins like lava. Slowly, he slanted his mouth over hers, taking her mouth in a deep kiss. He branded her with a sudden possessiveness he couldn't explain. She tasted like perfection, and her touch fed his addiction. He couldn't get enough of her.

Brad took her with him as he reclined on the mattress, settling so they faced one another. He continued to kiss her as he shoved her panties down, tossing them aside. Pulling her leg up over his hip, he opened her to his touch. He slid his fingers into the wet heat of her core, stroking her sensitive flesh, absorbing her soft sounds of pleasure with his mouth. His cock expanded, throbbed in response to her arousal.

As if she'd read his mind, felt his urgency, she said, "Get undressed."

"You love giving orders, don't you?" But he wasn't ready to do her bidding. Instead, he dipped a finger insider her, and began a slow rhythm back and forth.

She gasped with the touch, her hand going to her face. "Brad." Impatience laced the word. "You're driving me insane. I want you."

He continued his teasing, fingers caressing her inner wall, loving how her hips moved with his hand, arching against him.

"You have me," he told her. "Don't you feel me, Amanda?"

Her lashes fluttered and then lifted. "No. I mean… yes." A soft moan. "I meant…I want…you. Inside me."

And with the words, she gave him what he wanted most. Her admission of desire. Why this was so important to him, he didn't know. "Not as much as I want to be inside you," he murmured, stealing one last kiss before shoving his pants down his legs. He was urgent to return to her, to feel the hot, wet heat of her take him in.

Amanda touched him everywhere. His arms. His chest. His stomach. Her hand circled the hard length of his cock, and he ground his teeth against the fire it evoked. Her fingers played along the tip of his cock, sending shock waves of sensation through his body as she spread the slick wetness there, an erotic form of torture given that he was so ready for her.

With a guttural groan, he pulled her close. His fingers tangled into the strands of her hair, his mouth slanted over hers, desperate for another taste of her. He savored the tantalizing sweetness of her tongue brushing across his, the flavor of her so addictive. He lifted her leg over his hip as he'd done before, filling his hand with her ass as he angled her body to his, settling his cock between her legs. A groan of pure pleasure escaped him as he nestled his hard length in the slick wet heat of her core.

"You feel so damn good," Brad murmured, his lips traveling down her jaw, her neck, her shoulder. He simply couldn't get enough of her. "I need to be inside you." His teeth scraped her shoulder. "Now."

"Yes," Amanda said, her voice raspy. Full of urgency. She reached between them, her hand circling his shaft. "Now."

"Wait." Brad's hand slid over hers. "Birth control."

"Pill," she said. "And I don't sleep around."

Her gaze went to his, as if in question. "I always wear a condo—"

He lost his words as she slid his length along her core, readying her body, teasing them both with how close they were to joining. He released her hand, all thoughts of birth control gone.

The room filled with the sound of their breathing, with the sizzle of anticipation. Her skin was hot against his. So hot. So perfect.

Body taut and ready, he couldn't bear another moment of waiting. He positioned his cock and entered her. One deep thrust and he sunk deep to her core. Amanda cried out, her fingers digging into his shoulder. For several seconds, they stayed that way, foreheads pressed together, bodies joined. Lost in each other. Feeling emotion with each breath they took. Intense. Potent. What flared between them went beyond simple sex.

Brad moved first, his hand sliding up her back, molding them together, as if they were one. It wasn't close enough. He wasn't deep enough. Wild need flared inside him, but he held himself in check. No rushing. He didn't dare succumb to the demands of his body. Not yet. She wasn't where he wanted her. Wasn't quivering on the edge of orgasm.

He began a sensual rhythm. Not just hips moving, but their entire bodies. Kissing. Touching. Tasting. Fully engaged sex until she was as wild as he was. Until they simmered. Until their movements became frenzied.

And Amanda demanded more.

She pushed him until he was on his back, clearly not satisfied with facing each other. She straddled him, wasting no time before she started to ride. Hips bucking against his, she slid back and forth, side to side. Her hair teased his face, his neck, his chest. She was beautiful. As wild as he had wanted her. On the edge, driven to tumble over. His hands settled on her hips, guiding her, helping her reach for more. Helping her find that perfect spot she sought. And he knew the moment she did. He could feel her muscles contracting. Taking. Felt her move faster. Harder.

She cried out. "Oh. I... Brad, I..." But she never finished the words. He felt her first spasm of release and the jerk of her body that followed. Then her orgasm rippled, grabbing at his cock, pushing him over the edge he'd been clinging to. He lifted his hips, pumping them upward as he pushed her down to meet his body. Once. Twice. Three times and he felt the rush of release, spilling himself inside her. Shaking with the intensity of white-hot lightning ripping through his body.

They collapsed together, pressed chest to chest, exhausted. Satisfied. His hand slid over her back, into her hair, and he found himself smiling. He couldn't remember the last time sex had taken him so far. Couldn't remember any woman ever drawing him into a challenge that felt so completely absorbing. And one thing was for sure.

Sex with Amanda had only made him want more.

10

AMANDA LAY DRAPED across Brad, little shock waves—the aftermath of her orgasm—still shooting through her. She could stay here forever, blissfully sated after the best sex of her life.

Nothing had prepared her for how intense this night would be. For the potency of her response to Brad. She'd thought once would be enough. But what woman would stick to such a proclamation when the sex was this good?

In the distance, a low sound registered in the back of her mind, but she ignored it, savoring the last bit of pleasure dancing along her nerve endings. Reveling in the feel of Brad's hand stroking her back, her hair. The man knew exactly what to do, and when to do it. But the hum became louder, more insistent.

"Amanda," Brad said, his mouth near her ear. "Your phone. It could be about your car."

"Oh, crap," she said, sitting up, instantly alert. How had she forgotten about her car? She slid off Brad and tried to grab the comforter to cover herself, but Brad was on top of it. In the midst of her struggles, her cell stopped ringing. Amanda let out a frustrated breath. "I need my car."

She headed across the room for her phone, nudity

forgotten as her mind raced with worries. Worst case, she didn't get the replacement vehicle and she'd have to take a cab to work. She doubted the paper would cover both the rental costs and cab fare, which would no doubt cost a fortune.

The bedside phone rang. Amanda sprang into action, climbing back onto the bed and crawling over Brad. He grabbed the receiver and handed it to her.

The front desk informed her she had a visitor, a rental agent. "I have to get dressed," she said. "I need about ten minutes."

She handed the phone back to Brad. "They brought my car."

"I figured as much. I'll go take care of it so you don't have to get dressed." He started to get up.

Her response was instant panic as she grabbed his arm. "No!" But even in her current state of urgency, she managed to get distracted by his delicious body, her gaze flickering down those sculpted pecs and nicely defined abs. She cleared her throat. "You can't go for me."

Brad's expression hinted at irritation. "Why not?"

"What if someone sees you?" she asked, and then felt a bit guilty. After all, he was trying to be polite. "Not that I don't appreciate the offer."

He stared at her, those too-blue eyes unreadable. "No problem, sweetheart." He propped himself against the headboard, and stretched out his long legs in front of him. "Glad to kick back and let you do all the work."

She felt confused. And irritated. On one hand, she liked his chivalry. On the other, she didn't like his quick change of mood. It seemed as though his charm lasted only until he didn't get his way. Didn't he understand that she could rescue herself? She didn't always need him riding in to save the day. Plus, what if someone did recognize him coming out of her room? Yes, it was a remote possibility, but it would be a disastrous one.

Amanda clenched her teeth. "Think about someone like Jack finding out about us, Brad. He'd rip me to shreds over this. In fact, it wouldn't surprise me if he ripped you along with me, given the right angle. Word would get around. And just how much respect do you think your teammates—or any professional athlete, for that matter—would give me if they thought I screwed people to get stories? I have a lot to lose." Her words were strained despite her best effort to hide how emotional she suddenly felt. She didn't want to regret this night, and hoped he didn't make her.

Shoving off the bed, she didn't give him time to respond, hating the fact that her clothes were all the way across the room. Suddenly, she felt more than naked. She felt exposed.

With a detour to the bathroom, she grabbed a towel and a little privacy. She did a quick job of cleaning up, then inspected herself in the mirror, finding her hair in disarray, her lips swollen. Her eyes looked a bit drugged, satisfaction rooted in their depths.

The man knew pleasure—that was for sure.

She grabbed an extra towel and headed back to the room. She tossed the towel at Brad, who remained where she'd left him. Still gloriously naked. Evidently, he had no intention of getting dressed. Furthermore, he appeared to have every intention of watching her as she did.

She gave him a look, intending to protest his ogling. But his eyes danced with mischief, and one dark blond eyebrow arched in challenge. An amazing thing happened. She smiled, amusement replacing her anxiety. Okay, maybe her reaction was over the top for the circumstances.

Lifting her chin, she decided to meet his dare. She dropped the towel, then began to dress, as if it were no problem at all that he watched. First she slipped into her skirt. Then her bra and shirt. Her shoes. Damn. Where were her panties?

"Looking for these?"

Amanda's eyes went wide as she found Brad holding her silk undies by one finger. She rushed forward, issuing a reprimand. "I have to hurry. They're waiting for me."

When she reached for her panties, he yanked them out of reach, his arm circling her as he pulled her across his chest. "Let them wait a little longer."

Her pulse kicked into double time as the warmth of his body seeped into hers. A bit of laughter escaped her lips despite her best effort to stop it. She schooled her features with determination. "Brad. I have to go."

"Not until we get something clear," he said.

She glared at him. "What?"

"I would never do anything to jeopardize your career. I just wanted to help you. I'm trying damn hard to clean up my reputation, too. As I'm sure you know, my contract is almost up and I don't want trouble any more than you do."

He said the words with so much sincerity, she felt herself go soft inside, the tension sliding away. "I—I guess I overreacted." On impulse she ran her hand over the sexy stubble on his jaw. "I'll be right back." She reached for her panties.

He yanked his hand out of reach again. "I like you

better without them." Their gazes locked, desire spiking between them. "Leave them off and think about what I'm going to do to you when you get back to the room."

A tiny ache began to build between her legs. The man had just given her an amazing orgasm and already she was wet again. She was curious what he had in mind. "And what exactly would that be?"

He smiled, and brushed his lips over hers, his hand sliding under her skirt, and over her bare backside. The touch transformed that little ache into a big one as his fingers dipped intimately lower. More of this and she'd demand he do her right now.

His teeth nipped her bottom lip. "Let your imagination run wild, sweetheart," he said. "I promise I will."

The phone rang again and she jerked back. "I have to go." Damn. He had to stop distracting her. She needed that car.

She tried to push away from him, but he held her close, ignoring the ringing. Ignoring her urgency. And just when Amanda was sure Brad couldn't do anything to blow her away any more than he already had, he did.

THE HOTEL ROOM DOOR shut, leaving Brad alone with his thoughts and the growing pain in his arm. He'd watched Amanda's face when he'd told her he cared about her job. He'd seen how much it meant to her.

He let out a breath and ran a hand over his head. What should have been a simple round of sex to win the bet and deliver a serving of humble pie to the rookie just got more complicated. Now Amanda was his secret and he'd have to find another way to put Becker in his place.

As for Amanda, Brad would have to ensure she never found out about the bet because he was nowhere near getting his fill of her. He doubted one night would even begin to do the job.

He swung his legs over the side of the bed and pushed to his feet, forcing himself to put his clothes on. It was going to be a long, hot night, and he needed Advil. Even though she knew about his injury, he'd prefer to down the medication in private and his stash was in the truck. His ego wouldn't let her see how right she was about his arm.

He actually needed something stronger than over-the-counter, but that entailed a doctor's visit and he couldn't trust anyone local. Lord only knew which doctors were cozy with team management. That meant he had to wait for the Texas series to see someone he knew would keep his secret.

By the time he tugged his shirt over his head, his arm felt like a lead weight. Amazingly, when he'd been buried deep inside Amanda, he'd tuned out the pain. Judging from the spasms darting from his shoulder to elbow, he was in for a rough night.

Brad was ready to go before he realized his predicament. If he left this room, Amanda would freak, afraid he'd be recognized.

Until he'd heard Amanda's concerns about Jack and her career, Brad hadn't given much thought to the scandal an affair between them might create. When he'd entered into this bet, he'd been so ready to smash the kid's giant ego, Brad had forgotten to think it all the way through.

He accepted the inevitable. He wouldn't be getting that Advil. Instead, he headed for the room service menu. He needed sustenance. He dialed the operator and ordered a broad selection of food. He didn't know what Amanda liked, but he was determined to make sure she was satisfied. In all ways possible.

IT TURNED OUT exchanging vehicles was a huge ordeal involving far too many forms to sign. At least thirty minutes had passed since Amanda had left Brad in the room, and she was more than a little eager to get back to him. The whole time she'd been filling in information, her imagination had been in overdrive. She could think of all kinds of naughty things Brad might do to her. And then there were the things she planned to do to him.

A fast swipe of her key card and Amanda was inside the room.

Alone.

Brad was nowhere in sight. His clothes were missing from the floor. Her chest tightened at the emotions rolling inside her. He left her? Without saying a word?

Her gaze slid to the closed bathroom door just as it opened, displaying a now fully dressed Brad. Amanda sucked in a breath at the sight of him. His shoulders filled the doorway. A snug T-shirt hugged the rippling muscles of his torso, tapering down to a trim waist. His powerful legs were covered in soft denim. The man had a body to die for.

"Hey," he said, giving her a one dimple smile.

No rejection in that smile.

She let out a breath, relieved in a way she didn't want to begin to explore. "Hey."

He started toward her and her heart kicked up a beat, her body humming with the anticipation of his touch. "I ordered room service," he announced, pulling her close.

Amanda grinned, his spicy scent teasing her nostrils. His strong arms surrounding her. "You read my mind."

Before she could ask what he'd ordered, a knock sounded on the door. "I guess that's it."

A few minutes later, Amanda rolled the second huge tray of food to the side of the bed where Brad sat waiting for her. "Did you order the entire menu or what?" she asked incredulously.

"I was hungry." He positioned her between his splayed legs. "Still am. Just not for food. Not when I know you've been walking around without any panties." His hand snuck beneath her skirt. "Were you thinking about what I was going to do to you when you were talking to the rental agent?"

Not that she'd admit to. "No." Her breath caught as his hand moved along the crevice of her backside, lower, lower, fingers intimately touching and teasing her sex.

"Liar," he whispered, leaning forward and claiming her nipple with his teeth right through her clothing. She gasped with the contact, her nipple pebbling with the rough pleasure he delivered. Resting his chin between her breasts, he stared up at her with simmering heat blazing. "You know you were."

He didn't give her time to respond, apparently determined to deliver on his promises of pleasure. One minute she was standing, the next she was on her back on the mattress, her legs over Brad's shoulders, skirt to her waist. The warmth of his mouth closed around her clit. The gentle sucking and teasing sent her into a haze of pure pleasure, just as he'd promised.

A real man of his word. And Amanda liked a man of his word.

THE SOUND OF Amanda's cell phone ringing drew Amanda from a warm, half sleep on top of Brad's chest.

God, what was it about phones tonight? She was exhausted. After Brad had eaten dinner, he made her dessert. Several times.

Amanda glanced at the clock and saw that it was two in the morning. Didn't late-night calls always deliver bad news? Her heart kicked at the thought of someone being hurt. She crawled across Brad and grabbed her purse from the floor, digging out her cell.

Amanda frowned as she noted the unknown caller ID. She punched the Answer button. "This is Amanda."

"Amanda." A sniffling sound. "It's…" Sniffle. "Laura."

Laura? Amanda thought a moment before it dawned on her. The groupie who had a thing for Tony. She turned away from Brad, feeling a bit awkward. "Hi, Laura. What's wrong?"

"Nothing. I just… Tony went home with that other woman."

The news didn't surprise Amanda at all. "I'm sorry."

She wasn't sure what else to say. From the few conversations they'd had, she got the impression Laura had a distorted perception of her relationship with Tony. She seemed to think there was more to it than sex. From what Amanda had observed, Tony wasn't encouraging Laura or promising any loyalty to her.

"I'm tired of the way he treats me," she said. "The things I could tell you, Amanda. Big things. I could hurt him so bad."

This wasn't Amanda's method to get a story. Relying on sources such as this one—ex-lovers with revenge on their mind—often bit a reporter in the ass. "You're upset. I think you should wait until you calm down a bit. Once you cross certain lines or betray certain confidences, you can't ever go back."

"I don't need to calm down. I know exactly what I'm doing. And if you don't want to talk to me, there are plenty of other reporters who do."

Namely, Jack Krass. Amanda thought of him cozying up to Laura earlier tonight and figured he'd been trying to gain her confidence, not get laid. That realization added pressure because it suggested he thought Laura had information to spill. The reporter in Amanda wanted that information before Jack, even as she felt uneasy. Talking to Laura about Tony somehow betrayed him and Brad, who was listening to her side of the conversation. What a mess. This was precisely one of those situations she'd wanted to have a plan for before having sex with Brad.

"Okay," Amanda said, buying time, trying to think of the best way to handle this. "Why don't we meet for coffee in the morning?"

"Tonight."

That one word held enough conviction to give Amanda pause. If she didn't do this, there was no telling what Laura would do. Still, Brad was here and Amanda barely knew Laura. She could be spouting nonsense, Jack's interest aside. "Coffee in the morning. Name the time and place."

Amanda grabbed the notepad and pen on the nightstand and scribbled down the directions. "Now, promise me you won't do anything until we talk." After getting Laura's agreement, Amanda ended the call. She tossed the pen down and stuffed the directions and her cell in her purse.

"Meeting someone in the middle of the night is dangerous."

Amanda found Brad standing up, already dressing. Regret settled in her stomach and she yanked the covers to her neck. "You heard the arrangements. We're meeting in the morning."

He stared at her, his expression hardening. "With Laura. To get a story."

Amanda stiffened, her fingers digging into the blankets. She could appreciate he'd feel protective toward his teammate, so she refrained from snapping a retort. "No. Not for a story. I'm going to listen to what she has to say but that doesn't mean I'll print it. I've given you no reason to distrust me," she said, her tone even. "In fact, just the opposite."

"Because you say you aren't going to tell everyone about my arm?" he challenged. "We made a deal for that silence, remember? Tonight stays private and so does my injury."

"You think that's the only reason I'm not telling? Didn't we already have this conversation? I could have exposed you before tonight."

Long moments of silence passed. He crossed his arms in front of his chest, his stance aggressive. "Groupies are trouble," he said, ignoring all of her points. "*Laura* is trouble."

"She's a kid who needs a friend."

"She's trouble. Walk away from this."

"I can't turn my back on her. She's upset."

"Can't or won't?"

"Brad—"

"If you print anything she says without the facts to back it up, Amanda, you'll never get another interview in the Rays' locker room."

Amanda swallowed, feeling a bit sick. "I'd defend myself but it seems I've already been convicted."

He didn't respond, didn't even glance in her direction. Amanda watched as he finished putting on his clothes. He'd shut her out before he'd gotten out of her bed. He tossed her a brief goodbye, then left.

She pulled her knees to her chest. Why was Brad so fearful of her getting close to Laura? Amanda couldn't help but wonder if Kevin's suspicions about Tony were true and Brad knew it. Maybe Brad feared Laura did, too.

The situation was complicated and her emotions weren't helping. The way Brad had turned on her hurt like hell. He hadn't listened to a word she'd said after Laura called. What was Amanda to take from his behavior? Was she a groupie to him and now that he'd had her—not to mention a surefire guarantee that she'd never print a word about his injury—he was tossing her aside? The idea stung given that she'd thought they'd shared more than sex.

Damn, she should have waited until she'd worked through all of the consequences of sleeping with Brad. She could kick herself for not giving this more thought. But, no. She'd let lust beat out logic. And look where it landed her—her career resting in the hands of a man who didn't trust her and a heart that felt a little too bruised for a one-night stand.

What a mess.

11

REACHING FOR the takeout coffee cup perched on the edge of her desk, Amanda took a sip. She winced at the bitter taste of the too-strong brew. It was 8:00 a.m. after a night of too little sleep and no matter how bad the flavor, she needed the caffeine. She'd gotten up early to meet Laura only to have her leave a message canceling while Amanda was in the shower.

Since she was already awake and not likely to return to sleep with Brad on her mind, she had come in to work. Focusing on her computer screen, Amanda ground her teeth and hit the Delete button. Her column ran tomorrow and it needed to be brilliant. So far she wasn't off to a great start. She had an idea, but not the spin that really made it edgy.

"Coffee has arrived." Reggie held two grande Starbucks cups.

"Oh, my God, I love you."

He grinned. "White mocha or caramel macchiato. I'm fine with either."

"White mocha, please." He handed her the cup and she took a long sip. "That is so good."

"I'm addicted," Reggie confessed. "I swear they drug the stuff. Some say Starbucks is a cult, you know."

"Cult? You're kidding."

He gave her a serious look. "They say the drinks have some special ingredient that makes you want more."

She wasn't quite sure she'd heard right. "You're telling me you believe an entire chain would drug their coffee."

"Something makes it addictive," he said, his expression still dead serious.

She shook her head in disbelief, staring at him as she searched for mischief and found it. "The drug is called caffeine and I'm a willing addict. And until I've had mine, I suggest you don't give me a hard time."

Reggie started laughing. "All right, all right. I'll go easy on you the rest of the morning." He grabbed a chair from the cubicle beside hers and sat. "I figured you'd need a boost after a night at the bar. So. Tell me everything."

Amanda took another sip to break eye contact so he wouldn't figure out *everything* amounted to more than she was willing to share. "Well, let's see. Jack was an ass, as usual."

Reggie snorted. "Tell me something I don't know."

"Here's an interesting subject. One of the groupies was hanging all over Tony."

He made a face. "Like I said, tell me something I don't know."

"Will you just wait? I'm getting to it."

Reggie took a drink as he waved her on.

"She was hanging all over Tony but he was more interested in another woman," Amanda continued. "I didn't think much about it at the time. But a couple of hours after I left, she called me."

"And?"

She detailed the call and the cancellation that

morning. "Needless to say, I'm tired and frustrated. Part of me was glad she pulled a no-show. I don't like the idea of getting a story through an ex-lover and that's how this is feeling. And this is so bad—" she hated admitting this out loud, hated what the competition was doing to her "—but another part of me worried she went to Jack instead."

"I doubt she went to Jack. He has a way with the guys. Women are another story."

"I can vouch for that."

"You're in a spot, though. How you handle anything Laura tells you will be delicate. You don't use it and she clams up, never telling you another thing and passes the word to everyone she hangs with. You do use it and it pisses off the team, then they won't talk to you. And that's presuming she's telling the truth. Nasty all around."

"You don't mince words, do you?"

"Nope, I do not. A wingman tells it like it is. But he also brings coffee. And on really rough mornings, chocolate doughnuts."

"I'll hold you to that," she said with a smile. "And it just so happens that I've been thinking about exactly this subject. The way I see it, if I get this steroid story and go to the player and give him a chance to tell his version, then I'll earn trust rather than destroy it."

"Sounds like a plan. The key is to beat Jack to the story. Despite what I just said, I think you have to work Laura."

"I know. I don't want to, but I will. Since we have a game tonight I'll try to catch her at the stadium. Until then I need to work ahead on feature ideas."

Reggie pushed to his feet. "Check. Reading between the lines—get lost."

Amanda grinned. "Yes, but only after I've used you

thoroughly. I need the best action shots of Brad and Casey pitching you can get me." She mentioned several other photos for potential stories. With so much performance pressure, she needed options in case she changed her mind.

Reggie winked. "You got it. I'll e-mail you the shots within the hour."

BRAD'S BOOTS scraped against the floor of the home-style restaurant where he was meeting Tony and Kurt for breakfast. He felt as rough as he probably looked. The ache in his arm had rendered shaving impossible. The pain, which radiated from his elbow to his shoulder, had kept him awake most of the night. That, and thoughts of Amanda.

He'd been a damn fool to align himself with a member of the press. That phone conversation with Laura had been a wake-up call. Amanda may not have sideswiped the team with bad press yet, but Jack had proved that once a reporter, always a reporter. They were all after a story. How they used the information they were given depended only on their current agenda.

The worst part of this situation was he still wanted her. If he ever found himself alone with Amanda, he wasn't so sure he could resist her. One night with her hadn't come close to satisfying his desire. She was in his head, working a number on him. Driving him insane.

Shoving away the thoughts, Brad approached the table, slapping on a game face.

Kurt grabbed his hat from the seat next to him, and stuck it under his chair. "Morning," he murmured, scru-tinizing Brad before adding, "Or maybe not."

"Long night?" Tony asked, as he buttered his toast.

Brad's only reply was a grunt as he sat. He prayed Tony wouldn't start needling him over Amanda. Most of the time Brad found Tony entertaining and could give as good as he got. This wasn't going to be one of those times.

A fifty-something waitress appeared beside Brad. "What can I get you?"

"Coffee. Black. And keep it coming."

"Something to eat?"

"Just the caffeine for now."

"I'll take some Texas Pete," Kurt said.

The woman stared at him as if she had no idea what he was talking about. Kurt asked every wait person at every restaurant for the Texas condiment, knowing they wouldn't have a clue what it was. Something in their reactions amused him.

"Hot sauce," Brad told the woman. She shook her head, then left to fill the order.

Kurt turned a sharp gaze on Brad. "You really are foul this morning."

Brad didn't reply, just turned his cup right side up so he'd be ready for his coffee.

"Guess you didn't get lucky last night, after all," Tony taunted.

"Like I'd tell you if I did." Brad thanked the waitress as she filled his cup. He brought the cup to his lips, eager for the brew.

"Becker sure thought you did," Kurt commented. "You should have seen the look on his face when he realized you and Amanda disappeared at the same time. That was one pissed-off preppy."

Tony piled eggs onto a piece of toast and chuckled.

"Yeah, he was and I loved it. As much as I enjoy watching that kid get you worked up, I enjoy seeing you do it to him ten times more." He eyed Brad. "But it's pretty damn clear something went wrong. What the hell happened?" He shoved the food into his mouth.

Brad narrowed his gaze on Tony. "You tell me. I just happened to be around when Laura called Amanda." He paused to let the words sink in. "Called crying over you, claiming to have some big secret you wouldn't want exposed."

"Laura." Tony's face went pale. He dropped his toast to the plate.

"Shit," Kurt said. "What's she got on you?"

"Nothing." Tony shook his head. "This doesn't make sense. I was with Laura last night."

Kurt's eyebrows shot up. "That wasn't Laura you left with."

Tony gave a slow nod. "I met up with her a little later."

"Two in one night?"

Tony didn't respond to Kurt. "It was damage control."

"Which wouldn't be needed if you weren't playing with fire," Brad said. The words were directed at himself as much as Tony. His time with Amanda had certainly been playing with fire. "Laura was ready to hang you out to dry last night. For all you know, she might have."

"Again," Kurt said, "what's she got on you?"

Tony's voice took on a defensive tone. "I told you. Nothing." He tossed his napkin in his plate. "I need to go. Doc's expecting me."

"There's one more thing you might want to know," Brad said, delaying Tony's departure. "Jack's asking questions."

Tony visibly swallowed. "What's new about that?"

"He says someone on the team is juicing." Brad made the statement in a flat tone and let it hang out there with implication. "He brought up your name."

"Same story here," Kurt said. "He cornered me last night. What happened to that guy? He used to have our backs—or so we thought. Now I don't know."

A muscle in Tony's jaw jumped. "That sorry bastard."

"I told him in no uncertain terms to back off," Brad said. "But Tony, man, watch your back."

"Yeah, Jack's after blood," Kurt added. "You can almost smell his lust for a big story."

"I agree," Brad said. "Jack is after the bigger fish. He wants to go national. That has to be it." He repeated the words his father had told him too many times to count. "So I say, keep your friends close and your enemies closer." What about Amanda? Was she a friend or an enemy? It didn't matter, because he couldn't afford to keep her close.

"Right," Tony said. "So we know what he's up to. That makes sense." He checked his watch and pushed to his feet. "I gotta go. Check you guys later."

Brad gave him a quick nod then watched him leave. Beside him, Kurt said what was on Brad's mind. "He's about to shit his pants."

"Yep," Brad said, leaning back in his chair. "Something's not right, that's for sure."

Kurt maneuvered his chair to the end of the table so he could see Brad better. "I've seen a lot of guys make stupid decisions with less on the line. So now that Tony is gone, what happened last night with Amanda?"

Brad could trust Kurt. Still, he sidestepped the real question. "I was mad when I heard her talking to Laura."

"You can't hold that against her," Kurt said. "It's her job."

"Reporters haven't exactly been friendly to me."

Kurt smiled. "You two looked pretty friendly last night on that dance floor."

"Yeah, well, I had Becker breathing down my neck about that damn bet. I almost forgot how dangerous reporters can be."

"I guess Becker can have her, then."

Brad shot him a go-to-hell look. "Stop trying to piss me off and eat your damn breakfast."

Kurt chuckled and reached for his plate of untouched pancakes. Personally, Brad saw nothing to laugh at. Because the truth was, thinking about Becker anywhere near Amanda tore a hole in his gut.

If things were different, he'd find a nice secluded spot, strip off her clothes and get lost in her lush curves. His groin tightened thinking about all the things he would do to her. If things were different.

12

DRESSED IN a simple blue dress and high heels, Amanda bypassed the press box to sit closer to the action. Her attire was meant to keep her cool in the sticky L.A. temperatures. A tough order, considering she was feeling some real heat. It was the third home game since the Nashville away series and, at the rate she was going, it would be the third game she'd been shut out by Brad and Tony. Neither one of them would talk to her.

Oh, she'd see Brad eyeing her when he thought she wasn't looking, but talk to her? Give her an interview? No way.

Somehow, she had to convince them to talk to her. They were key members of the team and her columns would start to suffer from their silence. As it was, Kevin was pressuring her to get the steroid story before Jack. It didn't matter that her readership was growing. The man was obsessed with beating Jack.

Which meant she had to take action tonight. Somehow, some way, she had to set things right.

Her gaze traveled to the field, seeking out Brad yet again, the sizzling awareness she felt for him was driving her crazy. Like a magnet, he drew her attention, her admiration.

Amanda stuffed a piece of gum in her mouth,

wishing it was a big fat nacho. Though she'd moved into her new duplex while the team was out of town, she had yet to find a nearby gym with a pool. She hadn't done her normal morning three-mile swim in almost a month now, so she had to watch her diet. She hated it because she liked to eat way too much.

Reggie sat beside her and changed the lens on his camera. "Warning. Don't look, but Laura is to your right several rows over."

Amanda cringed. Laura had been calling her constantly since the morning of the no-show. She would ramble about Tony, clinging to Amanda like a long lost friend.

"Please don't let her see me," Amanda said. "I don't know what to do about her. And I'm sick of her dangling this apparent secret about Tony in front of me." Amanda regretted having gotten to know the groupies. Aside from those first few tidbits, they hadn't provided her with any inside tips to follow up on. And it seemed their hanger-on tendencies extended to the press, so they were hard to escape. "I'm getting all kinds of warning bells with Laura. Something is not right with that girl."

"You could cut her off. Tell her you don't have time for her calls," Reggie suggested, resting his camera on his knee. "But you risk her secret going to Jack. And if that secret is the steroid story, you risk big trouble with Kevin. I still wonder if Laura really has a secret at all. She could be working you, girl. Maybe she gets off on it. Maybe she's doing the same kind of thing to Tony."

"I was wondering that myself." This was so not how she'd seen her career playing out. She hadn't signed up for secrets and manipulation, yet she'd backed herself into this corner. "Based on the cold shoulder Tony and Brad are giving me, if I don't cut her off, the team isn't going to trust me. What if more of the players stop talking to me?"

Reggie opened his mouth to answer but stopped short when Laura obviously spotted her. "Amanda!" She was standing up waving her hands.

"Oh, man," Amanda said. "Right in front of the team."

"You could pretend not to see her," Reggie offered.

"Amanda!"

"Right," Amanda said. "The way she's screaming the entire world knows she's calling me." She gave in to the inevitable. "I'll be right back."

Amanda joined Laura and listened to ten minutes of Tony stories, before she made an excuse to leave. She started to turn when the tingling sensation of being watched took hold.

She searched for the source, instinct guiding her to the edge of the dugout. Her eyes locked with Brad's. She inhaled sharply, taken aback by the unexpected connection. The coldness of his gaze reminded her of that night in her hotel when he'd shut her out. Obviously, he'd seen her with Laura just now and he was judging her the same way he had that night. Damn it, she didn't deserve his wrath. Still, underneath her anger she felt a pinch of unease she didn't want to analyze.

Frustration danced along her nerve endings and Amanda wanted to scream. She barely knew Brad. He shouldn't hold anything over her. She had to put an end to this standoff tonight.

The sound of a bat cracking against a ball broke the

spell. Amanda tracked Tony's ball as it sailed across the field and flew over the back wall. That home run not only would win the game, but also bring him within a few home runs of his record. It was a press-worthy achievement, one she needed to report and Tony wasn't even speaking to her.

Resolve formed. She was going to take control again and those two had better be ready to talk.

AFTER THE GAME, Brad walked into the locker room with Kurt. Brad's mood went south the minute he saw Becker talking to Amanda. He ground his teeth, every muscle in his body tense.

"Becker wants to win that bet," Kurt said. "You gonna let him?"

Brad jerked his locker open and grunted. "He doesn't have a chance in hell." Truth was, the bet had long since been won. Too bad he couldn't tell anyone.

"Because you already won, right?"

"Stop digging. That's a reporter's job."

Amanda's laughter filled the air, wreaking havoc on his nerves. Brad glanced over at her, taking in the way her face lit up as Becker talked, as if whatever he said was really interesting.

"Sure looks like Becker's giving it a rookie try," Kurt said, twisting the proverbial knife. "Maybe he's going for a tie."

"Cut it out, Kurt. I'm not in the mood." He grabbed a towel. "I'm going to take a shower." Before he spewed the curses he'd been biting back.

A few dodged reporters later, Brad stepped beneath the hot spray, hoping to escape the scurry of activity and pull himself together. But there was no escaping tonight.

Becker stepped into the stall next to him, on the hunt for a fight.

"Damn man, Amanda is hotter than hot," he said. "I'm going to thoroughly enjoy winning this bet."

Brad suppressed his claim of victory. If he heard Becker call her *hotter than hot* one more time, he might throttle him. He so wanted to make sure Becker never went near Amanda again.

In his current mood, Brad was a ticking bomb that needed to be far away from Becker, and he knew it. He turned off the flow of water and wrapped the towel around his waist. But he couldn't walk away without saying something. "You should concentrate on throwing the ball into the mitt, kid," Brad said. "Because if you keep pitching the way you did tonight, you won't be around long enough to get Amanda in bed."

He left, humming over Becker's yelled retort. Brad made it to the main room only to be cornered by some guy wearing a bow tie and a press pass from the opposing team's home paper.

"Was that Casey Becker yelling at you in there? That have anything to do with that fight you two had back in Ohio?"

"It wasn't a fight," Brad mumbled, and tried to sidestep and retreat.

The guy blocked his move. "Looked like a fight to me."

Brad was losing his patience. "Okay, then. It was fight."

Success flashed in the guy's beady eyes. "I thought so. What were you fighting about?"

The coach walked out of his office, propping a

shoulder on the door frame. His eyes locked with Brad's, a silent warning evident in his expression.

Brad turned back to the reporter. "Why'd we fight? The kid likes Pepsi. Me, I'm a Coke guy." He shrugged. "What can I say? We ballplayers get pretty intense about our cola."

Coach let out a roar of laughter, and relief rushed over Brad. He maneuvered around the less-than-pleased reporter, this time with success. Inwardly, he kicked himself for stepping in the line of fire, even though he'd averted disaster. Did he need reminding how important avoiding trouble was to his contract renewal?

And that trouble included Amanda. The thought only served to rekindle his foul mood.

LONG AFTER the game ended, Amanda waited near Tony's car, Reggie by her side. She was ready to clear the air with Tony. Ready to put this Laura issue to bed and open communication with him again. Maybe she'd even be lucky enough to get a quote about tonight's home run.

There was just one problem. When Tony appeared, he wasn't alone. Brad and Kurt flanked him.

Fine. Amanda had to face not one, but three, very big, very intense ballplayers. Judging from the scowls they wore, they weren't pleased to see her.

She tried to resist squirming beneath their glares. Of all the eyes upon her, the ones who dealt her the most discomfort were Brad's. She could feel his scrutiny scorch her skin. But she refused to look at him. Refused to forget that this meeting was about Tony, not Brad. She would not be deterred from her goal.

"Showtime," Reggie said. "How do you want to play this?"

Amanda pushed off her rental car, which she'd moved to this parking lot. Her purse was on her shoulder and she left her notepad inside. She wanted to keep this easygoing and off-the-record.

"Solo, but don't go anywhere. I need the moral support."

Reggie winked. "I'll be here."

Walking toward Tony's red Porsche, Amanda noted how different he was from Brad and Kurt. While the other two men wore jeans and T-shirts, Tony sported designer pants and an expensive button-down shirt. Brad's good ol' boy quality was nowhere to be found with Tony. Everything from Tony's attitude to his car seemed to scream big city and big money.

Amanda's hope that Brad and Kurt would go their way and leave her alone with Tony proved to be unfounded.

"Hi, guys," Amanda said, waving her hand then focusing on Tony. "I wanted to talk to you." She paused. "Alone."

Tony stared at her, seconds passing in silence. The streetlight above seemed to cast her in the spotlight while she waited.

"I promise I'll only take a minute." Amanda responded to the resistance she spotted in his dark brown eyes. "I don't want to miss the chance to report on that big home run."

Finally Tony seemed to relax. "All right. I guess I can give you a couple of minutes."

"Great." She turned to Kurt. "Maybe I can catch up with you at the next game?"

He tipped his hat back, giving her a direct look. "Depends. You gonna start traveling with us?"

Amanda had decided to be straightforward with the

team, so she explained the situation. "If my boss likes my next story, then I'd say yes. If not, I might be headed back home to Texas but not for the game."

"Oh, man," Kurt said, hands sliding in his front pocket. "Being a rookie is never fun."

"It has its moments," she said, then forced her attention to Brad, not about to let him think she was intimidated. "You still owe me an interview."

His eyebrow inched upward. His expression was unreadable but still managed to suggest intimacy. "Do I?" he asked. "I thought we covered just about everything last time."

The private, underlying meaning charged the air. Amanda swallowed against the sudden dryness in her throat, finding herself at a rare loss for words.

"Not everything." That was the best she could up with in front of an audience.

"She asked to talk to me," Tony said, moving his chin to dismiss the other two players.

Saved by Tony's need to be the center of attention. His interjection rescued her from a mess with Brad. Plus, she'd guaranteed his willing participation by asking to speak to Brad and Kurt.

The three men exchanged a few words, then Amanda found herself alone with Tony. Arms crossed in front of his body, an expectant look on his chiseled face, he confronted her.

Clearly, he was on edge, even though he wanted this interview. He wanted the attention but not the questions about anything beyond his home run.

"Tony, it's important to me to earn the trust of the team. I figure to do that, I need to shoot straight," she said, repeating the words she'd practiced in her head while waiting for him. Saying them out loud, however, she worried they came off as lame and insincere. "That's why I'm not going to print anything that could be damaging without talking to the player involved first."

His eyes darkened, the rich brown color becoming deep black. "What does that have to do with me?"

Touchy. She wondered why. "Maybe nothing," Amanda told him, "but sticking to the commitment I just made, I want you to be aware of a few things regarding Laura. She's been clinging to me a lot, doing a lot of talking."

"So what?" he said, his tone clipped. "She's the social type."

"She's talking about you, Tony. She gets upset and cries, and threatens to tell some big secret."

"I don't have any *big secret,*" he said, hands going to his hips. "Whatever you're trying to find out here, it won't work."

"I'm not digging. And I'm not trying to find out anything. So far I don't recall asking a question." Amanda let her statement linger a moment for impact before she went on, choosing her words with care. "She hasn't confessed anything, and I don't push her to. Frankly, a jealous girlfriend isn't the best of sources."

"She's not my girlfriend."

"She thinks she is. I've seen you with her and I know you have made your lack of commitment clear. But she's not listening. She's young, Tony. She'll get hurt easily and lash out."

He turned away briefly and sighed. "I've never done anything but shoot straight with Laura."

"I believe you." Tony was proud of his well-earned

reputation with women. An apparent lover of variety over longevity, he never kept a woman around for more than a few weeks. "But that doesn't make this situation less of a problem. If she comes to me and shares this secret and I do nothing with it—assuming it merits a story—then she'll go to someone else. Maybe to Jack."

"Great. So this is a heads-up that I'm screwed."

His statement was telling. If he had nothing to hide, he wouldn't have said such a thing.

"What I'm saying is the most I can offer you is a chance to tell your side of things before it hits the press. I won't print anything she tells me without talking to you first. The thing is, I'm in a bad spot, Tony. If I pull away from her, I might not be the one she tells. That's another reason I came to you. I don't want you thinking I'm trying to work her. Frankly, I feel damned if I do, and damned if I don't."

A moment passed, then he gave her a slow nod. "I appreciate the position you're in and your willingness to come to me before printing anything."

She swallowed, hating the next subject. "There's one more thing."

He scrubbed a rough hand over his jaw. "Do I want to know?"

"Probably not and honestly I don't even want to bring it up, but—"

"Just say it."

"Okay," she said. "I'm following a lead about steroid usage on the team. I believe Jack is, as well. If he gets the story before me, he won't give any of you a chance to save yourselves."

She searched his face for a reaction and found none. No shock. Nothing. Maybe Tony wasn't her guy.

She shifted her stance, waiting for a response. When it didn't come, she said, "Just point the right people my way if you get the opportunity." Deciding to end on a positive note, she charged onward. "Heck of a hit tonight, by the way. How close are you to that record?"

Tony stared at her. Finally, his lips stretched into a smile, straight white teeth showing. "Two more."

Amanda grinned. "Amazing. So close you can taste it, I bet?"

He was quick to respond, talking openly about a subject he enjoyed. She followed with several more questions geared toward her next feature. By the time she said her goodbye, Tony seemed happy.

Now to the next challenge: Brad.

The sooner she talked to him and cleared the air, the better.

BRAD STOOD by his truck, watching Amanda talk with Tony. Beside him Kurt waited, as curious as Brad to find out what was going down.

"I like her," Kurt said out of the blue, hands settling on his hips.

"Who asked you?" Brad asked. He watched the animated way she moved her hands as she talked, her hair floating around her shoulders as it had that night at her hotel.

"You like her, too," Kurt commented.

Brad cast him a sideways warning. "Like I said. Who asked you?"

Kurt laughed, apparently satisfied he'd gotten whatever reaction he was digging for. Before he could launch his next smart-ass remark, Amanda and Tony parted and Tony headed their way.

"So, what's the damage?" Kurt asked as soon as Tony was within hearing distance.

Tony leaned against Brad's truck. "That was the strangest conversation I've ever had with a reporter." He shook his head. "I don't know what to make of it."

"Off the truck," Brad ordered. "You'll scratch the paint."

"It's a damn pickup truck and you're on it," Tony protested, not moving.

"It's mine and I can do what I want to it. We can't all drive Porsches."

"But you can drive a Porsche," Tony argued. "You chose a truck."

"I like my truck. Get off."

With a low growl, Tony pushed off the truck, hands in the air before they fell to his sides. "Do you want to hear about this or not?"

"Yes," Brad and Kurt said at the same time.

"She warned me about Laura. Told me about the phone call and other conversations she's had with her. Says she wants to earn our trust."

Brad snorted. He might think Amanda was hot, but he wasn't a fool. She was a reporter and almost all of his encounters with the press eventually turned bad. "In other words, Laura didn't tell her squat so she was trying to get the story from you."

Tony dismissed Brad's cynical remark. "I didn't get that from her. But her warning, on top of what you guys have been saying about watching my back, has me thinking. Laura's a problem and I've known it for a while now. Every time I pull away from this chick, she freaks out on me. And no," he added, fixing Brad in a direct look, "she has nothing on me."

This was where Tony's self-centeredness and his the-world's-all-about-me attitude backfired. He'd used Laura and it was coming back to bite him. "I told you to stay away from those groupies." Brad had been lucky that his days of sampling the groupie pool hadn't resulted in any scandals. No, his scandals all came from other places.

"Yeah, well, I can't do squat about what's already done. She can make shit up and I can't stop her. I'm working toward the biggest goal of my career and I don't want it overshadowed by gossip."

"And Jack has an agenda he's working. Watch your back with him." Brad could relate to Tony's dilemma. After that bar fight, legal issues and bad press had over-shadowed anything he did on the field.

"Yep," Kurt said. "You're knee-deep in shit for sure."

"Once you're that far in," Brad commented, "some-times you just have to say screw it and face the situation head-on. If it were me, I'd stay away from Laura. You can't let her hold you prisoner."

"He's right," Kurt agreed. "Cut it off now. The longer you wait, the worse the ending."

"I can't. Not this close to breaking my record. I don't need the trouble she could create."

Brad shrugged. "You've got to do what feels right." What else could he say? He pulled the keys out of his pocket. "I'm outta here."

"You're skipping the bar?" Kurt sounded surprised.

"Yep. Places to go. People to see."

"What's her name?" Tony asked, grinning.

Brad had already opened the door so he lifted his hand in farewell. There was no *her* but they didn't need to know that. The best way out of the game night cele-brations was to let them think he had a date.

And he did. With an ice pack and a bottle of Advil. The only woman on his mind was Amanda, and she caused almost as much pain as his arm. He didn't want to think about her. He didn't want to see her. So why was he sitting in his truck thinking about her?

He pounded the steering wheel with his good hand. "Get out of my head, Amanda."

With a deep breath, he started his engine, and faced facts. Amanda wasn't anywhere close to getting out of his head.

13

As he drove home, Brad still thought about Amanda. Almost halfway there, his thoughts managed to churn into suspicions. He had to confront her to make sure she wasn't jerking Tony around. Problem was, he had no idea where she lived. In some remote corner of his mind that fact registered as a warning he should stay the hell away from her. He ignored the warning and dialed information. Sure enough, she was listed. Name, number, address.

Fifteen minutes later, he stood outside her door, telling himself to leave. But he hesitated. He'd come to talk about Tony, hoping the secret between himself and Amanda would be ammunition to head off trouble.

Yet, if he were honest, he'd admit these were excuses. He'd come here because he simply couldn't stay away.

Without giving himself time to back out, he knocked. A few seconds passed with no response and again he debated walking away.

"Hello? Who is it?"

"It's Brad."

Almost instantly, the door flew open, and Amanda appeared in the doorway, her face lit in panic. She still wore the sexy, form-fitting dress she'd had on at the game. The one that hugged her curves in all the places he wanted to.

Before he knew her intentions, she reached forward and grabbed his arm, yanking him into her house then slamming the door shut behind them.

Whirling to face him, she went on the attack. "Are you crazy?" she demanded. "I rent from the weather woman at the paper. She lives next door."

He wasn't used to embarrassing the women in his life and her outrage hit a nerve. "She didn't see me," he snapped. "I don't see why it matters."

"Of course, you don't. But it matters to me because—" She shut her mouth, cutting off her own words. "Why are you here? How do you even know where I live?"

"Finding you wasn't hard. You know, you might want to switch to an unlisted number, considering your job is in the public eye. And for the record," he added, "if you think I like sneaking around, you're wrong."

"Then you shouldn't have come."

A muscle in his jaw jumped. "I had to. Besides, no one saw me. I parked a few blocks away."

She didn't seem comforted by his words. "Why? Why are you here?"

Whatever he'd expected coming here, it wasn't this frustration. She was acting as though she was pissed off to see him and he found himself getting defensive and edgy. "We need to talk about this Tony situation."

Apparently not the right thing to say. If he'd thought she was upset before, it was nothing compared to what followed.

"Tony." Her tone was low and terse, as if she barely restrained herself from yelling. "To make sure I'm not screwing him, I assume? Well, I'm not. Contrary to your low opinion of me, I'm protecting him."

"Amanda, I—"

"In fact, I'm protecting him despite my boss's demands that I do whatever it takes to get the story before Jack. If my landlord sees you here, everyone will think that's exactly what I'm doing. They'll think I sleep around to get my stories. After all, people will reveal anything across a set of pillows." Her hands slashed through the air. "I've worked too hard to get that kind of reputation, Brad. Why didn't you just call? You've done it before. I know you know what a telephone is." She leaned against the wall, giving him free access to the door. "You should go."

Could he feel like more of a low-down dog? "Amanda—"

"Just go."

"I don't want to," he said. "I'm on edge and I know it. I was unfair."

"Yes," she said. "You were."

He didn't know what to say. Emotions he didn't understand or like burned in his gut. Damn it, she got to him, this woman. And he got to her. A need to hear her say as much pressed him to act.

He pinned her against the wall with his body, his legs framing hers, his hands on either side of her head. He was rewarded with the soft, flowery scent of her. He was addicted to that smell. No. Addicted to *her*.

"I want you, Amanda."

"You had me," she said, her hands pressing against his chest to maintain space between them.

"It wasn't enough."

"It has to be."

"Do you really want that?" he asked, knowing it wasn't. He could feel the slight give of her body as it softened into his. Her hands stopped pushing him away.

She drew a shaky breath. "You have to leave."

"I can't leave," he said, resting his forehead against hers.

"I can't do this, Brad." Her voice was low.

He eased backward a bit, letting her see the truth in his eyes. "I didn't come here about Tony. I told myself that was the reason. I'm really here because I needed to see you. Because I couldn't help myself."

"You said—"

"I lied."

Confusion flashed in her eyes before her expression hardened again. "You left my hotel room acting as if I couldn't be trusted. I've done nothing to deserve that. And now you admit you are the one lying? I don't want to play these games with you."

"No games," he said. "I can't get you out of my mind." They stared at each other, sexual tension building between them. "That's the truth."

"I don't know what to believe," she murmured. "I don't... We can't."

He leaned forward, resting his cheek to hers, relieved that she didn't push him away. She felt so good to him. He felt her inside and out. Felt her everywhere. What was she doing to him? He could barely breathe from the way her touch, her nearness, stormed his senses.

"Tell me to stay," he whispered in her ear.

"Brad."

"Tell me to stay." He forced himself not to kiss her, not to press more than he already had.

Her hand went to his face, a tender touch that tightened his gut. "This is so not good for either of us."

Her response spoke of acceptance and he responded. His lips slid along her jaw, brushing the sensitive skin with a long caress as he traveled. He absorbed the sweetness of her as his lips touched hers.

"Trust me," he whispered, his hands leaving the wall to cup her face as he stared down at her. "No one will ever know."

"Like you trust me?" she asked, her voice soft, full of passion, but her eyes alive with challenge.

The way she challenged him was arousing. "Trust is earned."

He brushed his mouth over hers, this time using his tongue to tease hers, barely sliding past her teeth for a quick, tantalizing taste. "We could start tonight."

"How exactly do you propose we do that?" she whispered, her mouth near his, their breath mingling. His hands slid down her neck, her shoulders, her sides.

"Every time you let down your guard," he said, "every time you trust me a little more, I'm going to reward you with pleasure." He let the promise linger in the air for several beats. "How does that sound?"

14

EVERY TIME you trust me a little more, I'm going to reward you with pleasure.

Amanda replayed the words in her head. How did that sound? It sounded like trouble. Like temptation. Like pure heaven.

Staring into Brad's eyes, Amanda processed the low hum of sensual energy inching through her body. Regardless of why he'd shown up here, only one thing seemed to ring in her mind. How much she wanted Brad.

He shifted, fitting their hips together, proof of his arousal pressing against her stomach, teasing her with thoughts of their naked bodies molded together in passion. Images of their earlier night flashed in her mind, tormenting her with what she might miss if she sent him away.

"What do you say, Amanda?" he asked in that deep, raspy voice that worked its way along her nerve endings. "Do I stay or go?"

His fingers inched her skirt up her thigh, his hand sneaking beneath the hem and scorching her bare skin. She swallowed against the sudden dryness of her throat. "You're rather persuasive."

His palm caressed the curve of her backside. "You

don't even know the half of it, I promise." He lifted her leg to his waist. His mouth lingered close to hers. "Tell me to stay."

"I already did," she countered, reaching for his mouth, only to have him pull back.

"No," he told her. "You didn't."

It was clear she wasn't getting kissed until she met his demand. Considering the delicious warmth spreading through her body, the price seemed a small one to pay. "Stay."

He smiled and slowly lowered his head. His lips closed over hers, his tongue engaging hers in sensual play. She melted into the kiss, into him, as a strangled moan escaped.

He seemed different tonight. More potent and forceful, yet, safer. He seemed to demand in a way that didn't command, but rather, invited submission. And, good lord, she wanted to submit.

As if he sensed her readiness, he ended the kiss and released her leg. "Turn around."

"Why?"

"Turn around, Amanda," he urged softly, his eyes dark with passion and challenge. "Trust me."

Why was she doing this? No answer came to her beyond the need to know what he would do to her. "All right."

Satisfaction flashed in his face before he leaned back enough to allow her to move. "Hands on the wall." He directed her as his palms settled on her waist.

The eroticism of the moment swelled. She couldn't see him, couldn't anticipate what he would do. Yet she could feel him, his body close, touching her in places that made her want more. She'd never experienced such a thing, her arousal so intense. She felt his hand on her zipper, easing it down her back. Already she ached for him, dampness clinging to the satin between her legs.

"I watched you tonight," he said, "standing across the parking lot wearing this dress. All I could think about was doing exactly what I'm doing right now."

His knuckles brushed her bare back, and she shivered against the unexpected touch. Molten heat moved through her limbs as if she'd been drugged, and her nipples puckered against their lace confines. He skimmed the dress from her shoulders, his hands following its path down her arms. She pulled her hands through the sleeves, letting it fall to her waist, then shimmying it down her hips. Her panties followed.

She stepped out of the pool of cloth, and he used his foot to widen her stance, opening her to his touch, to his stare. She stood before him, wearing only her bra and her high heels. Knowing he was fully dressed right now made her feel incredibly sexy, as though she was his to admire.

"You're beautiful," he murmured. The compliment fed the ache in her core, just as it had during their previous encounter.

He undid her bra and she shrugged it away.

"Hands back on the wall."

She didn't hesitate or argue. She wanted what he offered far too much.

His thighs aligned with hers, his cock pressing into her backside. His hands slid to her stomach, then burned a path upward until they covered her breasts. He sculpted them with his palms, his touch firm, yet gentle.

With his long fingers he tweaked her nipples, drawing them into hardened peaks, pleasure rippling through the sensitive buds.

"Does that feel good, Amanda?"

"Yes." She gasped as his fingers lightly tugged on her nipples. "Yes."

"See what happens when you trust me," he murmured, palming her breasts again and kneading.

Amanda moaned, finding herself arching into his hands even as her hips pressed backward into his erection, wanting all she could get of him. Never had she felt such abandon during sex. And she liked it so damn much.

His mouth touched her neck, and she leaned to the side to give him better access. She could barely breathe as his lips and teeth nipped, licked, teased. She started rolling her backside into his cock, desperate for him. As much as the scrape of his clothing against her skin tantalized, she hated the barrier of his clothes. Their presence indicated how long she had to wait to feel him inside her.

And when she thought she would scream with frustration, he seemed to sense her need building. He slid down her body, hands traveling her sides, her waist, her hips, until he was on the floor between her legs.

Reality rushed back to her. This position made her vulnerable, exposed. She stiffened, wanting to cover herself.

Before she could speak, he caressed her cheeks with his hands and lips. "Easy, sweetheart," he murmured. "Remember, pleasure. But you have to trust me."

His hand slid between her legs, his fingers claiming her swollen clit and teasing it. Amanda's breath caught in her throat at the action, her body again taking her beyond thought, beyond resistance. She was lost as his fingers slid through the dampness of her sex, gliding along her sensitive folds, pleasuring her even more than promised.

Tension built low in her stomach, demanding more, demanding she rock against his fingers. But as she pressed against his hand, he stole it from her reach. An objection on her lips, she gasped to find the wet heat of his mouth closing over her. He'd spun around so that his tongue could lap at her with delicious perfection.

With precision, he used his tongue, his mouth, his fingers, to stroke her, rocking as she rocked. That tension in her stomach knotted, built, pushed, and she cried out on the edge of release. In response, he steadied her with his free hand, supporting her so she wouldn't fall while he sucked her fully into his mouth.

Suddenly, her muscles clenched before a flutter of spasms delivered bursts of pleasure. The pleasure seemed to go on and on, taking all of her.

The last flutter passed, leaving the heavy leaden sensation of being sated and satisfied. "Oh, my," she said, laughing, almost embarrassed by how intensely she'd come.

Brad stood, picking her up as he rose. "Where's the bedroom?"

Amanda pointed down the hall and he carried her to the pitch-black room, pausing at the light switch so she could flip it. A second later, he laid her down on her bed, the white down comforter she'd purchased absorbing her body. Weight on her elbows, she watched as he pulled his shirt over his head and those broad shoulders and that perfectly sculpted chest came into view. Her eyes lingered on the sprinkling of light hair on his pecs, knowing it would feel delicious against her breasts.

She realized her satisfaction wouldn't be complete until she had him inside her. Until he was on top of her, that hard body braced above hers.

He pulled off his boots and she saw that she still wore her shoes. She shifted to remove them.

"Don't," he said. "The shoes are sexy." He spoke the words as he dropped his pants, his erection now in view.

This man packed an unfair amount of male beauty into one body and she'd do almost anything to get her hands on it. So if he liked the shoes, she liked the shoes.

He knelt on the mattress and before he could move farther, she grasped his hard length in her hand. Her gaze lifted to his, searching for his reaction, and finding the heat she sought.

She yearned to explore the effect she might have on him, but his hand came down over hers. "As much as I like you touching me, I need to be inside you right now."

He didn't wait for a response as he pressed her to the mattress, his body covering hers. His erection fit into the slick heat of her arousal as his mouth settled on hers, hot desire pouring through her as their tongues tangled in a wicked dance of need. Hungry. Passionate.

She curved her legs over his calves, arching upward, aching to have him fill her. She laced her hands through his hair, bodily holding him captive any way she could.

Tearing his mouth from hers, he left her breathing heavily, desperate for more, as he pressed upward, his powerful arms holding his body above hers.

He reached between them, took his cock in his hand and slid it along her core. Back and forth, he tormented her with what was to come. Her lashes fluttered with the whirlwind of sensation the movement created, wet heat pouring from her body.

"Look at me," he ordered. "I want to see your eyes when I enter you."

With supreme effort, Amanda did as he said, staring into his heavy-lidded gaze. The intensity of the moment robbed her of the ability to breathe.

The soft tip of his erection nudged her opening, and anticipation kicked her heartbeat into double time. She clutched his waist, holding on for the wild ride to come. And then it was there as Brad thrust deep.

Inhaling long and deep, Brad's broad chest expanded, drawing Amanda's attention. "You feel so damn good," he murmured in a husky tone. "So wet and hot. How do I feel, Amanda?" He pulled back, inch by slow inch, then he thrust again, hitting her core and setting off an explosion of pleasure. "How do I feel, Amanda?"

He wanted an answer and she was really trying, but the words wouldn't form, shyness rendering her speechless. It was crazy considering what they'd already shared. Still, no man had ever spoken so boldly to her. No man had ever demanded she vocalize her pleasure. But then no man had ever given her so much of it as Brad, either.

"Amanda." Her name on his lips pressed her to respond.

"I…good." Her voice had a breathless quality. "You feel…stop teasing."

His eyes lit with satisfaction. "I never tease." He thrust again, burying himself in her body, then he lowered himself so that her nipples nestled in the soft hair of his chest. He kissed her with the hunger of a starving man.

They started to move. A slow, seductive rhythm of bodies melting together, moving back and forth, side to side. Hands exploring, caressing, touching.

Amanda's head spun from the fieriness of their

shared passion. Nothing existed except this. Now. Brad. She felt herself slip into the fog of those feelings, of the pure need to be closer to him. To feel him deeper. More. She wanted more.

She arched, meeting the pump of his hips with her own, her kisses becoming as demanding as her body. Brad met each stroke of her tongue, taking her further under the spell with each taste. Each touch.

And when she thought she could take no more, he thrust hard, caressing her inner wall with perfect friction. His head went to her neck, her hands to his hair. A frenzied rush of movement followed. Thrust, pump. Thrust, pump. Until the ache of being so very near release had her rocking, hips off the bed, afraid of losing that one perfect spot. He seemed to understand, his hands sliding beneath her, palming her butt, as he anchored her, held her steady.

Together they moaned as he lunged deep. Once. Twice. And then she exploded, her muscles grabbing at his hard length, milking him for their mutual pleasure. He pumped into her one more time, then his body stiffened before shuddering.

Slowly, their bodies softened into satisfied bliss. Time passed as they remained in that embrace. Amanda wasn't sure how long. She only knew that she had just had the best sex of her life. And there was something else. Lying here naked, cradled close to Brad, felt comfortable, like a place she never wanted to leave.

Before she had time to give that idea any consideration, Brad lifted his head, resting his weight on his elbows. "I have a serious question for you."

Uncertainty made her heart skip a beat. "Yes?"

He tilted his head slightly, as if he was giving her closer inspection. "Are you hungry?"

She blinked, not sure she'd heard right. "What?"

"Are you hungry?"

"I…uh…" Her stomach actually felt empty, though the question seemed oddly timed. After all, the man was still inside her. "Yes. I'm hungry."

He smiled. "Good." Satisfaction showed on his face and he gave her a quick kiss. "Because good sex always makes me hungry. I figure if you're hungry, then it was good for you, too."

Amanda shook her head in disbelief and started laughing. "You're kidding."

He frowned a bit. "It was good for you, right?"

How could he even question such a thing considering what they'd shared? Still, a part of her warmed that he had asked. That he hadn't assumed she'd been into it.

"You know very well it was good for me," she told him.

"A guy can never be too sure." He rolled off her, and started to get up, then returned to kiss her. "And since we are putting things on the record tonight, I take good sex and food quite seriously." Then he smiled. "Let's order takeout."

Pushing to his feet, he gave her a great view of his nicely shaped butt. He headed to the bathroom, completely comfortable in his nudity. Only a moment later, he settled back on the bed and handed her a towel.

While he reached for the phone book by her bedside, Amanda started to get up, searching for her robe. Brad reached for her arm. "Where are you going?" he asked. "We have to figure out what we want to eat. Unless you want me to order a little of everything like before?"

"God, no. Don't do that." She laughed. "Give me a minute. The air conditioning is blowing right at me and I need a robe."

He grabbed his shirt from the end of the bed. "Put this on."

The intimacy of the gesture shook Amanda. Wearing Brad's shirt, ordering takeout. All these domestic customs were what couples did, not people having a one-night—or in their case a two-night—stand. The contentment she took from these actions was really scary.

She accepted the shirt. Her nostrils flared with the spicy perfection of his scent as she pulled it over her head.

Then Brad tugged her to his side, and placed the phone book between them, asking her what she wanted. Lord help her, she knew the answer.

She wanted Brad.

15

BRAD SAT ON THE BED next to Amanda, take-out containers from one of his favorite restaurants—a twenty-four-hour joint that served everything under the sun—spread out in front of them. He had pulled on his boxers when the food arrived, though he planned to discard them the minute they were done eating. Amanda still wore his shirt, but she'd added shorts to answer the door. Those would have to go, too. Soon.

He enjoyed Amanda's company far more than he'd expected to, which only made him hotter for her. Funny how that worked. A guy could want a woman only to have the attraction fade when she opened her mouth. With Amanda, the opposite was true. Just ordering food had proven fun. They'd debated several choices, and compared likes and dislikes. She hated fish and so did he. They both loved sweets. And morning coffee, for both of them, came before conversation.

He reached for his chicken sandwich and took a bite, fighting the ache of his arm. Their little sexual adventure had aggravated the pain. That made him pathetic that he couldn't do a round between the sheets without his arm protesting. Despite the ache, he had no intentions of leaving.

The truth was, he had no time for a distraction like

Amanda. His career was hanging by a thread and he needed to stay focused until management ponied up a deal he could sign. And after what had gone down in this big bed tonight, he knew Amanda would claim attention he couldn't spare. Still, he wasn't leaving, consequences be damned.

Finishing off a bite of his food, he watched her spray extra whipped cream on top of her half-eaten strawberry waffle. The intense look on her face said her task was very important. A cute little wrinkle appeared between her eyebrows as she concentrated. She made the cutest faces.

"I might have to order one of those," he commented, having passed on the waffle for the protein boost of the sandwich.

Amanda eyed his plate. "I don't know how you'll have room. That is the biggest chicken sandwich I've ever seen."

"Never underestimate my appetite," he warned, thinking of how hungry for her he was. "Maybe I'll just use the whipped cream on you." Brad watched her reaction, surprised to see her face color. "Are you blushing?"

"No." Guilt flashed on her features. "Okay, maybe a little."

When was the last time a woman he'd dated actually blushed? He found Amanda's mix of innocence and vixen sexy. As sexy as the sight of her in his T-shirt. He'd given it to her for a selfish reason—so that he could enjoy that sweet floral scent of hers on the drive home. He was a sap.

He decided to spare her blushes and changed the subject. "Your dad and your sister are both doctors but you aren't. How did that happen?"

"I have a little problem with blood." She stabbed a strawberry with her fork. "But I love the sports part as much as they do. So when I couldn't compete anymore, I started reporting."

Brad didn't even want to think about what came next for him. Deep down, he knew he needed to, though, especially if no contract materialized. But somehow, planning for that future seemed to be admitting his ball-playing career was over. How was he supposed to give up the only thing he'd ever wanted to do?

"I'm sure it's not the same." How could watching from the sidelines ever be as amazing as playing? Hell, his off nights made him crazy having to sit in the dugout and think about how he'd play each scenario differently. The only thing that got him through those games was knowing he'd be pitching his turn in a matter of days.

She tilted her head and studied him. "At first it's hard, but not forever."

He thought she would say more, talk about his future, but she didn't. Yet, he sensed she was telling him this for his benefit.

A change of subject was needed. "And your mom?" he asked. "What does she do?"

"She teaches kindergarten. I have a doctor and a teacher for parents. Talk about protective."

He snorted. "Try being in high school and having both of your parents teach at the school. I couldn't make a move without them being on me about it."

"I'll bet," Amanda said, with a short laugh. "Your dad coached, right?"

"Yeah," Brad said. "I hate that he never saw me make the majors." He suddenly realized who he was talking to. Amanda was a reporter, and this wasn't casual pillow talk. "This isn't an interview, is it?"

Her eyes flashed with irritation before she looked away, pushing her plate out of reach as if no longer hungry. "Okay. So conversation is out. Forget I asked a question."

He grimaced then exhaled, hating the way she'd erected an instant wall. Hating that he'd made her do it. "Amanda." Brad considered his words. "I've been burned by the press. More than once. And right now I have a lot on the line."

She fixed her attention on him, her green eyes sharp as they settled on his face. "So do I, Brad. Burning bridges and creating enemies isn't going to help me, either. You came here tonight spouting about trust. You ask for it, but apparently you aren't willing to give it."

He was a shit to make her feel they couldn't have a conversation. Worse, there was a thread of truth in her words. "What happened with you and Tony tonight?" he asked, because he needed to clear the air. To make sure she deserved his trust.

To Brad's surprise, she didn't hesitate to answer. "I warned him about Laura," she said, facing him. "If she has something on him, she'll use it. I think it's just a question of when."

He narrowed his eyes on her. "Why would you warn him? You're a reporter."

A frustrated sound escaped her. "You surprise me, Brad."

"What's that supposed to mean?"

"You label reporters like we're some sort of demon race capable of only bad deeds, like there's no individuality. I guess I could do that with pitchers. Maybe I should assume you and Casey are the same type of person."

"Me and Becker?" He snorted. "You have got to be kidding."

"You're both pitchers," she said. "Aren't you all arrogant and immature?"

He had just been put in his place. Laughter rolled from his lips as he hugged her. "I stand corrected. Not all pitchers or all reporters are made the same." His lips brushed hers. "Forgive me?"

"Well, I guess I'll cut you some slack since you're in pain."

"Pain?" he asked, leaning back to face her. "What are you talking about?"

"You haven't used your throwing arm since we started eating. Even now it's plastered to your side." She trailed her finger along his top lip. "And you have this white line here. You're hurting and don't tell me otherwise."

Reluctantly, he nodded. "Okay. I'm hurting."

"How long until you have to pitch again?"

"Just practice the rest of this week. If the rotation holds, I pitch at the end of the next series. Then we're in Houston before Dallas and I think Coach will bench me those games to save me for the Rangers. There's minimal throwing in a long stretch of games so I should mend."

She shook her head. "You need more time than that and we both know it. When are you seeing a doctor?"

"In Texas. After the series."

"You don't even have an appointment lined up yet." She made a frustrated sound and pushed out of his reach. "Every time you pitch injured, you risk permanent tissue damage."

"Every time I don't pitch, I risk permanent career

damage. I risk my contract with the Rays." He hesitated. "I moved my mom here last year, so it's important I stay with this team."

She didn't say anything for a while, and he expected her to come up with an argument of some sort on why he was the world's biggest idiot gambling with his arm. But he expected wrong. Without another word, she got off the bed and located her phone.

"My sister is as good as they come. And she's discreet. She actually treats a lot of baseball injuries. I'd like to call her and let you two set something up."

Brad was stunned by her offer. Where were the lectures about telling his coach or his agent? Where was the pressure to take himself out of rotation? And why wasn't she taking notes for her next column? He felt vulnerable—a wholly unwelcome emotion—as his preconceived ideas about her toppled. Maybe she was genuine. Maybe he could trust her.

"All right, then," he said.

A hint of a smile curved her lips as she dialed. A few seconds later, he listened to her laugh and joke with her sister before detailing his situation. "Yes. I'll tell him about Daddy."

Finally, she wrapped up her conversation. She covered the mouthpiece with her palm before offering it to him. "Her name is Kelli. She's the wild one in the family, just so you know."

He wasn't sure what to make of that, but he nodded and accepted the phone. "Hello. This is Brad."

"Bradley, sweetie, this is Kelli. Listen, we're gonna get you all taken care of. I'd feel better if you were seeing the doctor who did your surgery, but I won't waste my breath and pressure you. We both know you won't listen. You're scared shitless over your career and that's guiding your decisions."

Brad laughed at the pure audacity of the woman. If anyone else had told him what she just said, he would have hung up. But the smoothness of her delivery backed up by an obvious confidence that she knew what she was talking about, make it okay with him.

Kelli continued, "So. Talk to me. Tell me about your previous injury."

"I don't know that this injury is related. Before my hand tingled and got numb. They said the nerve needed to be repositioned."

"An ulnar nerve transposition. Does that sound right?"

"Vaguely familiar. I didn't catch the details."

"Hmm. Don't remember anything other than when the doctor said you could play again. Most of my patients suffer selective hearing. I'm working on a cure. Back to you. Now you say your pain is more localized, your elbow swells and you have tendinitis-type symptoms."

"Right. Exactly. So what does that mean? How bad is it?"

"I can't tell you that from a phone call. I'll meet you after hours the night you get into town and arrange some tests. Anyone I enlist will keep my secrets, trust me. Hopefully, before you pitch another game I can tell you how much damage you're doing to yourself. I can also give you some medication to help the pain and inflammation. I assume you're taking Advil and using ice?"

"Right."

"And you made up some story to get out of practice this week."

He knew he should, but that would raise flags he

didn't dare risk. "No, but I plan to dodge pitching as much as possible."

"It would be better if you skipped it altogether and hopped on a plane to come see me now. But I know you aren't going to do that. Just be careful."

They talked a few more minutes and scheduled the meeting. "And Brad," Kelli said. "Do yourself a favor. Find a good acupuncturist right away. They can't cure you, but they take away some of the pain."

"An acupuncturist." Surely he'd heard wrong.

"Yes. Listen to your new doctor. She knows best. I've never lost a man, yet, sugar, and I don't plan to now. Put my sister back on the line."

Amanda took the phone and talked for a bit before hanging up. "Well then," she said. "You're all set. Kelli said to stop second-guessing her and go to the acupuncturist."

"I wasn't—"

"She says you are."

He laughed. "Okay. I was."

"She has a unique approach, but her patients love her. Most doctors don't pimp vitamins and herbs the way my sister does."

"I can't wait to meet her," he said. Not because Kelli interested him, but because everything about Amanda fascinated him.

She hesitated. "There's one thing you should know beforehand, though."

"Do I want to know?"

"This is kind of embarrassing. My dad is a huge fan of yours. If he finds out you saw my sister and he didn't get to meet you…" She shook her head and crinkled her nose. "Let's just say it won't be pretty."

"Isn't he an NFL team doc?" he asked. "I figured he'd be more into football than baseball."

"He loves all sports, but baseball is equal to football. And you're his favorite player. Kind of weird, huh?"

"I'm flattered," Brad said, sincerely. Knowing he had fans always made him happy. "I'd be happy to meet him."

"He'll want your autograph. He collects them." She rolled her eyes. "No. Chases them. He's obsessed." She laughed. "At his last birthday party, he wanted everyone to sign a banner. He'll milk any opportunity to add to his collection."

"Does he sell them or something?"

"Oh, no," Amanda said, waving off that idea. "He has them all displayed in a huge room. He wouldn't dare part with a single one."

"He sounds like quite the character," Brad commented.

"Yes. I'm definitely the normal one." She rose and headed toward the bathroom.

A few seconds later she reappeared, a medicine bottle in hand. She popped a couple Advil into her palm and held them out to him.

He accepted the pills and reached for a drink. As he swallowed, his gaze settled on the front of his shirt, on the way Amanda's nipples puckered beneath the material. Desire rushed through his veins, hard and fast.

As soon as he swallowed the medication, he reached for Amanda, pulling her between his legs. With his index finger, Brad lightly traced one plump nipple before tweaking it to a stiff peak. "I want you."

She sucked in a breath. "That's not a good idea. You're hurting."

Brad grinned. "Then I guess you better be on top."

16

NAKED AND LYING on her stomach, Amanda blinked awake. She brushed her hair off her face, and took in her surroundings. Daylight registered first. Next, the spicy scent of male cologne. Images of her and Brad making love played in her head. She barely remembered falling asleep.

She lifted her head higher but could find no sign of Brad. The distant sound of running water grabbed her attention. He was in the shower, which made her wonder what time it was. She eyed the clock, panicking when she saw it was well past her usual wake-up time.

She kicked off the blankets, then darted for the bathroom. She had to get ready in half her usual time.

Not bothering to knock, she shoved open the door. She pulled aside the shower curtain and climbed in. Thank God, the water was hot.

Brad's eyes went wide at the sight of her, then a sexy smile spread across his face. "Morning."

She swallowed hard at the long and lean sight of him. And though she tried not to—she didn't have time to dally—her eyes slid down his abs and even lower to notice he was quickly getting hard.

She moaned at the thought of having to ignore such

an invitation. "Change places with me. I'm late. I have to get to work."

He let her maneuver into his position, then he grabbed the bottle of soap from the side of the tub. "Let me help."

"No!" she said. "Step back, Brad. I'll never get to work if I let you distract me. Better yet, get out."

He laughed and leaned against the wall. "I'll keep my hands to myself and just watch."

Watch? Amanda felt the water pour over her shoulder. The temperature wasn't warm enough to explain the heat suddenly coursing through her body. And it certainly wasn't cold enough to make her nipples tighten and ache the way they did. No. Those reactions were all compliments of the erotic sensation of Brad watching her. Making love to her with his eyes as he had with his body.

By the time she finished in the shower not ten minutes later, she was wet in more ways than one. It didn't help that Brad watched her dress while he wore nothing but a towel. How would she ever look at that man in a towel again and not develop naughty thoughts?

Thankfully he left her alone to dry her hair. She was putting on makeup when Brad poked his head into the bathroom. He now wore his jeans, which hung low on his hips, but nothing else. "How do you like your coffee? I saw creamer and skim milk in the fridge."

He made coffee for her? Amanda's heart squeezed at the gesture—another one of those domestic touches that made them more a couple than just lovers.

"Skim milk would be great," she said, feeling a flutter in her stomach as their eyes met.

He winked. "Coming up."

He brought her a cup. Amanda accepted it and took a sip. "Perfect. Thanks."

They stared at each other for several intense seconds, the sizzle between them beyond physical. There was more. Amanda felt it in every inch of her body, inside and out.

He cleared his throat. "I guess I better let you get ready," he said.

"Right. Yes. I need to hurry." But what she wouldn't give to blow off work and spend the day playing in the sheets with Brad.

WITH ONE EYE on her watch, Amanda headed out the front door only to discover Karen's car parked in the driveway. Damn. She needed to warn Brad not to leave until Karen had gone. The last thing she wanted was Karen finding out who'd had a sleepover next door.

Amanda was about to go inside when her gaze caught on the paper. She had finally printed her story about Casey. She'd included a comparison of his stats to Brad's. What a coincidence that Brad was here the morning it hit the stands. She snagged the paper then darted back into the house only to have the door fly open. Brad, now fully dressed, stood in the doorway. "Hey," he said, offering her a charming smile. "I thought you left."

She rushed at him, shoving him into the house and letting the door slam behind her. "Karen hasn't left yet. She could see you."

"Like she'd care. She's the weather woman, Amanda. Has anyone ever told you you're paranoid?"

"I don't want anyone making assumptions about me. Stay here until she's gone."

"You run around naked in front of me and tell me I can't touch. Then you act like I am worse than the plague because no one can see me. I have to tell you,

Amanda, this isn't the kind of reward a man expects after a night of great sex."

"No, it's the punishment for overstaying your welcome."

His lips twitched with an ill-contained smile. "You don't mean that and we both know it."

"You're very arrogant, Brad Rogers. And since it's public knowledge, don't be surprised if I write about it."

"Apparently you like arrogant."

Now she was fighting a smile. "When I said all pitchers were alike, I didn't mean it." She shoved the paper at him. "Interesting enough, in today's feature I did a little comparison of you and Casey."

"What?"

She laughed. His expression said he was imagining all kinds of horrible things the story might say about him. "Stop panicking. I went easy on you. But now who's paranoid?" She shook her head. "I'm going to work." She headed for the door, pausing to peek at him over her shoulder and wave.

Stepping onto the porch, Amanda decided she enjoyed being the one with the upper hand. She headed for her car, cell phone in hand.

She punched in Reggie's number and the minute he answered she started talking. "Reggie. Oh, good. I got you. Please, please, please cover for me. I know I'm late but I—"

"Slow down, honeybun." Reggie laughed. "You're a reporter. You don't punch the clock."

Amanda got into her rental. She'd be so glad to have her own car back. "I know, but—"

"No buts about it. However, I have some interesting news."

Don't let it be about me and Brad. "What news?"

"We're going on the road, baby! Kevin called me into his office this morning to say I was tagging along for your first time out."

"You're kidding? We're going on the road! I'm not getting fired."

"No, you're not getting fired." He sounded exasperated, as though he were getting tired of reassuring her.

"Well, not yet at least. As long as Jack doesn't bust out with the steroid story before I get to it."

"Stop ranting about Jack. I have more news."

"More?"

"Yes, more. Good news, too. But I'll tell you when you get here. I think you should pick up doughnuts on your way in to celebrate."

"Oh, you do, do you?" She grinned from ear to ear because she couldn't seem to stop herself. "Whatever you know and haven't told me yet better be good."

"Oh, it's good," he said with confidence. "Éclairs. I like éclairs."

"Fine. But I need directions to the location of these éclairs. And later you can direct me to a good gym to work off the two I'm going to eat myself."

Amanda took down directions and then started the car. A hot night of sex and great career news—what more could a girl ask for?

Just as she pulled into traffic, her phone rang. She hit the answer button without even checking caller ID. "This is Amanda."

"You accused Becker of wearing garters?"

Brad's deep voice sent a shock wave of awareness through her body. "I did not. I simply said there are rumors he's a *Bull Durham* fan with similar superstitious habits to the pitcher in the movie. I went on to say he denies anything of the sort."

"I'm sure he'll see it that way."

"Maybe Casey has a better sense of humor than you."

"According to the stats you listed, it's all he has better than me."

"He fares well against your stats when you were a rookie." Brad snorted. "Ah," she said. "You're a little touchy when it comes to Casey, I see."

"Not at all. I just don't like the kid."

"At least you're honest."

He changed the subject. "I think you should invite me over tonight."

Amanda was thankful to pull up to a stoplight because his words caught her off guard and left her more than a little rattled. A couple of nights of sex was one thing. But spending two nights in a row together was leaning toward a relationship. And no matter how much she wanted him, she couldn't have him. At least not without jeopardizing her career.

"We had a one-night stand. Well, two nights, but regardless. That means we don't see each other again." Disappointment settled in her gut as she said the words.

"But we will see each other again because of your job. Why not work the sex out of our systems? If we have so much sex we don't want each other anymore, then there will be no chance we'll give ourselves away."

Amanda laughed. Somehow she doubted she'd ever work sex with Brad out of her system. "You think that's possible?"

"Be fun to try."

Yeah, it would. "But dangerous. We both have a lot to lose if anyone catches us together."

"You're right." Pause. "How about tomorrow night?"

She should say no. She told herself to say no. Instead, she said, "This is insane, Brad."

"I have a pool. You can swim."

A smile touched her lips. "Bribery is so unfair."

"I never claimed to be fair," he said. "Just honest."

"That you did." His offer was so very tempting.

"You know you want to," Brad said. "And you owe me. I waited until Karen left before walking to my truck."

"Okay. Fine. What time?"

"Do you have my number in your phone?"

"Hold on." Amanda checked to be sure. "Yeah. I got it."

"Good. Call me before you go to bed and we can make plans. You can tell me a naughty bedtime story while you're at it." The line went dead.

Amanda hung up and took several breaths, trying to calm her racing heart. Oh, God. She was so falling for Brad Rogers. She didn't just lust after him. She actually liked him. But what future could they have? If anyone found out, it would really affect her professional image with the team. She should tell Brad no when they talked later that night. Better yet, she shouldn't call him.

But she knew she was going to call him. And she knew she was going to see him. She couldn't seem to help herself.

"I GOT THE ÉCLAIRS. Now talk." Amanda fixed Reggie with a challenging stare as she set the box on her desk. "What other news do you have?"

He reached for an éclair but she pulled the box out of reach. "No eating until you start talking."

He sighed. "Has anyone ever told you you're very demanding?"

She crossed her arms and tapped her foot. "Reggie."

"Okay. Okay. Kevin arranged for us to travel with the team on their private jet. I'm sure I don't have to tell you how rare that is. Not even Jack Ass flies in the team jet. This should really get his panties in a wad."

"Really? I can't believe it."

"Yep. And that's not all."

"More? What more could there possibly be?"

"Kevin mentioned another piece of news while I was in his office. Are you familiar with *L.A. Woman?*"

"Remotely. I think it's a lot like *Dallas Woman* in Texas."

"I don't know about that. But I do know *L.A. Woman* is big here. Apparently one of the editors reads your columns and is intrigued by your take on things. She wants to book an interview. Kevin seemed quite pleased. Well, as pleased as Kevin can ever seem."

Amanda's mind was racing, her excitement hard to contain. "When? What kind of interview?"

"That's all I know. You'll have to see Kevin."

"I need to just back up and calm down. I don't want to get too excited. Maybe it's not that big a deal."

"It is a big deal. But before you go getting all happy, I took a call from Becker you need to deal with. He's pissed."

"Any specifics on why?"

"The garter thing seemed to be the focus of his rambling."

She pursed her lips as she thought of her conversation with Brad. "I didn't say he wore garters. I said he didn't."

"Funny how some guys can get so sensitive," Reggie said.

Amanda gave him the evil eye, then she claimed the box of éclairs. She needed a sugar fix and at least two cups of coffee before she called Casey.

Sucking up took lots of energy.

17

TWO GLASSES OF WINE in his hands, Brad watched Amanda finish a lap in the pool, knowing she had two more to go. He'd watched her swim every night for a week, loving every minute of being in the water.

He sat at the edge of the pool, setting the glasses on the pavement beside him. He was content to sit here and enjoy the night. The temperature was reported at ninety-plus, but his pool overlooked the ocean, and the evening breeze swept in from the water, delivering soothing coolness.

He wasn't sure what Amanda was doing to him. All he knew was he couldn't get enough of her. Thankfully the team had had a string of home games and off days that kept him in L.A. These past two weeks with Amanda ranked among the best he'd lived in a long time. He told himself this was just about great sex. That she kept his mind off his injury. But truthfully it was more than sex. He'd talked to her more than he had any other woman.

A voice deep inside whispered a warning. He was getting too close to her. Too involved. He wanted another five years on the mound before he could even think about settling down.

Reaching for his wine, he took a sip, reminding

himself Amanda had a career to think about, too. She couldn't afford to be seriously involved with him any more than he could with her.

She swam his way, stopping in front of him. She settled her hands on his knees, sending heat through his veins. Amazing how one touch could set him on fire.

He stared at her, searching for what it was about her that got to him. The answer seemed everything. Water clung to her long dark lashes and her hair was slicked back from her beautiful features, accenting her huge green eyes.

"Hey," she said, smiling.

He set his glass down again and slid into the pool, pulling her close. "Hey, yourself." His mouth brushed hers, absorbing the droplets of water still clinging to her lush lips. "Hungry?"

She nodded. "Starved."

His gaze dropped to her pebbled nipples pressing against her light-blue bikini top. Brad slid his hands up from her waist, framing her breasts with his hands, before running his thumbs over the stiff peaks. "Me, too." He shoved aside the material and rolled her nipple, pleased when she sucked in a breath.

She reached up and covered herself. "Not until you feed me. I'm weak. You wouldn't want me to pass out on you, would you?"

He contemplated pressing her against the wall and taking her right here and now. He'd do all the work and she wouldn't have to do anything but enjoy.

"Oh, no," she scolded. "I know that look in your eyes. No means no. Feed me!"

Damn, she read him well. Caving to her demands, he released her and pushed up on the side of the pool, offering her his good hand in assistance. Once she sat beside him, he reached for the towels behind him and wrapped one around her shoulders.

"So what are we going to eat?"

"Pizza?" he suggested.

"Not chicken?"

He grinned. "Actually, I know this healthy place that makes fantastic pizza."

She rolled her eyes. "I should have guessed. So far everything you've said would be good has been, so I'll trust you."

Brad reached behind him again and grabbed the cordless phone. Once their food was ordered, they sat in comfortable silence, as they had on several occasions.

"Are you excited to be traveling with the team?"

"I am," Amanda said. "And I can't wait to see Jack's face when he realizes I'm invited on the team jet."

"You and Jack. You're like two dogs fighting over the same bone. Let him have it and make your own path. Otherwise this one-upmanship will eat you alive."

"I know. I'm trying. Right now, the pressure is from my boss, not Jack. He has me chasing a big story to get it before Jack does."

Brad's jaw tightened. There wasn't a ballplayer alive who liked the subject they were headed toward. "If you mean the way he's been sniffing out a steroid story, so is every other reporter alive. It's the hot topic everyone wants a piece of."

"Yeah," Amanda said. "That's what I meant. I figured Tony told you I was asking questions."

"I knew Jack was." Brad thought of Jack's accusations about Tony and prayed they were false. "He questioned me about some of the players and I told him to stick it."

"I'd have loved to have heard that." She kicked at the water, her expression thoughtful. "I'm not enjoying this part of my job. At first, when Kevin pressed me to go after this story, I didn't hesitate. I wanted to beat Jack. But now I realize Jack's agenda can't be the same as mine. There's no way to break this kind of story on your home team and still be allowed in the locker room later."

"You got that right."

"So why would my boss push me to get this story?" Amanda frowned. "Unless…unless that's his plan. Maybe he knows he'll have to replace me, so he'll get the goods first."

He ran his hand down her back, noting the worry in her face. "Your readership is growing. I'm sure that's not the case. He probably wants the story so much, he's not seeing beyond that objective. It happens. Besides, if someone is juicing—which I don't think is the case— it needs to be dealt with behind closed doors. Kids need heroes. What example does it set when they find out their hero is doing drugs?"

Amanda stared at him, her eyes lingering on his face, softness in her eyes.

"What?" he asked.

"I like you, Brad."

He laughed. "You like me? Good thing considering you get freaky with me."

"Oh, I don't have to like you to be in lust with you, but I do like you. You're a nice guy. Arrogant as hell, but still a good guy."

Brad kissed her. "Well, I like you, too, Amanda Wright. And I still want your body."

"You can prove it after you feed me. Hey, how was your second acupuncture appointment?"

Brad flexed his hand. "Good. I can't believe how much it's helped. That sister of yours has already won me over."

Amanda sipped her wine. "She usually does. My ex was a sports medicine doctor, too. He became obsessed with outshining Kelli but he never could."

Her ex had come up once before but the subject had been quickly changed. "That must have been tough on you."

She shrugged. "I guess it was. I feel like such a different person now. It's like the woman who married him and lived that life wasn't me. Hard to believe I was with him. Now there was a man with a God complex."

"God complex? Explain."

"According to Kelli, all doctors, pilots and athletes have massive egos and think the world revolves around them."

He snorted. "Correct me if I'm wrong. She fits that list."

"She says she doesn't count."

"Of course not. Funny how that works in her favor." He studied her a moment. "You think I have a God complex?"

"No, but I don't know if I'd recognize it. I didn't with my ex."

"Not really liking that comparison."

She grinned. "Sorry. Casey fits the God complex. Tony certainly does. Kurt…I haven't talked to him enough to decide."

"Not Kurt. He's completely untouched by the spotlight. I respect the guy a lot."

"And Tony?" she asked. "You seem to be pals."

"Tony's entertaining. He has to come back to earth before I decide if I truly respect him. He's good and he knows it."

"He's cocky and arrogant."

"Exactly. But sometimes you have to be. The pressure is intense. The talk around you messes with your head. Sometimes you have to pump yourself up so they can't bring you down. And other times they're building you so big you can't even see reality."

"Sounds like experience talking," she said.

"You and I both know I took a public beating over that bar fight. I had to find my zone to overcome it. That meant believing I was better than everyone else. And it worked until I got hurt."

"What happened that night?"

Oddly enough, Brad didn't feel the need to dodge the question. He shrugged. "I was stupid. This U.T. pitcher started talking trash and I had a couple beers in me. The combination wasn't good."

"I don't get it, Brad. You were at the top of your game. What could the guy have said that set you off so bad?"

Brad ground his teeth. He hadn't told anyone what had really gone down between him and that guy. Figured it didn't matter. The end result was the same, no matter what.

"I knew him," Brad said, not sure why he was telling Amanda what he'd told no one else. "His older brother had played ball for my father."

"Oh, no." Amanda's words came out a low whisper. "Tell me he didn't trash-talk your dad."

Brad's chest tightened. The way Amanda knew things before he even said them amazed him.

"Yeah," he said, after several seconds of silence. Talking about this was helping in a way he hadn't known needed to be helped. "It was the anniversary of his death. I was feeling kinda edgy. My mom had been on the phone to me earlier that day and I heard how bad she was hurting. The timing, the alcohol… I let it get to me."

"And then he sued because you punched him."

"Right."

"You never told anyone this part of the story, did you?"

"That wouldn't have done anything but spread it all over the papers and upset my mom. And for what? In the end, I punched the guy. I was stupid and it bit me in the ass."

"I can't believe you kept this quiet."

"Becker reminds me of that damn kid. So much so that sometimes I want to punch him, too."

She surprised him by laughing. "I never would have guessed."

"That obvious, huh?"

"Just a little."

She was beautiful like this—natural, perfect. Brad tugged her close and pressed her hand to his crotch. "I want you."

"I never would have guessed," she teased, stroking him with her fingers.

The doorbell rang and he cursed under his breath. "I don't suppose you'd let me ignore that."

She smiled and gave him a quick kiss. "Not a chance."

AT 8:00 A.M. THE DAY the team left for Texas, Amanda stood inside the terminal of the private airstrip waiting to board the Rays' jet. Reggie was off getting her coffee and she loved him for it. She'd stayed up far too late the night before, and her body ached with the demand for sleep.

She wore black from head to toe—pants, cotton blouse, boots. Black traveled well. Amanda didn't.

Flying had never really been her thing. She got nervous over every bump, every sound.

It didn't help that she was nervous about being in such proximity to Brad, who had yet to show up. Would she be able to hide from the others how she felt about him? Or would they all guess she had fallen hard for their star pitcher?

They'd said goodbye last night agreeing to keep their distance on the road. Once they were back in L.A. they'd probably pick up where they left off. Or would they? They hadn't actually agreed to that. During this trip Brad could decide he'd had enough of her and never want to see her again.

God, she hated flying. It made her paranoid.

Still, they should stop their affair and use this time as the opportunity to do that. She had a job to think about. At the end of the day she wanted her career, not a longer fling with Brad. Right. That's exactly what she wanted and if her libido was thinking otherwise, she could ignore it. This wouldn't be the first time.

Reggie appeared by her side and handed her a cup of coffee. Casual as usual, he wore a Rays' ball cap over his dreadlocks. "Mocha straight up," he said. "The choices were limited. I had to get it from a machine."

"I'll take anything I can get," Amanda said.

Around them, players talked to the press and to family, saying farewells. Amanda kept her distance. She had two weeks of living day and night with these guys, so there was no rush to get close.

"What kept you up so late?"

"I didn't finish tomorrow's feature on Tony until near two. I was afraid to wait and have some sort of travel delay keep me from making deadline."

What Amanda didn't say was that she'd stayed far too late at Brad's, not going home until the last possible minute.

"My shots were okay, right?" he asked, sipping his coffee.

"They were perfect."

"And your headline?"

She grinned despite her tiredness. "The Italian Sweet Spot."

Reggie let out a bark of laughter that drew attention. "Oh, my God, that is too good. It's perfect. Of course, you mean the *sweet spot* as in the perfect place on his bat."

Amanda wiggled her eyebrows. "Guess you'll have to read my feature to find out." Of course, he was right about her meaning. Tony had talked quite a bit about *the sweet spot* on his bat during their interview. She felt his agreeing to talk to her showed she was earning his trust. "Once you get past his ego, he's a pretty nice guy."

"Seems Laura still likes him," Reggie said, moving closer and lowering his voice.

Amanda caught a glimpse of the couple. The atmosphere between them seemed strained as Laura spoke to him and Tony responded. Her expression indicated displeasure with his reply. Still, she pushed to her toes, and kissed his cheek.

"I've warned him," Amanda told Reggie. "He won't listen. You know, she hasn't called me in days. Not since I told her she should consider dating other guys. I know I shouldn't have said it, but I had a weak moment. She hung up on me."

Casey walked past them, and winked at Amanda.

"I swear, that kid is either mad at you or trying to get in your pants," Reggie muttered.

Amanda elbowed him. "Behave," she said. "He and Laura would be quite the mature pair, though, wouldn't they?"

An announcement over the intercom indicated they were ready to board. "Great," Amanda said, inhaling.

"Flying is safer than driving," Reggie reminded her for the fifth time since he'd arrived.

She cast him a warning look. "I told you to stop saying that. It doesn't help. I'm going to the bathroom so I don't have to get up on the plane."

"I'll wait on you."

Amanda eyed the signs but didn't see one for the bathroom. She looked left, then right. Right looked, well, right. But after passing several gates, she saw no bathroom. Worse, being a private airport, the customer service seemed limited. She was about to turn back when she heard Jack's irritating voice ahead. Strange. What was he doing down here? She should have noticed his absence at the gate.

She really didn't want to see him, nor did she want to eavesdrop. But for some reason, she was frozen in her steps. A woman's voice filled the air.

"I told you, Jack," Laura said. "I was mad when I called you. I don't have a secret to tell."

"He doesn't care about you, Laura," Jack said. "And I can prove it."

"What are you doing?"

Amanda jumped, surprised to hear Brad behind her. She whirled around, caught eavesdropping. He wore soft Levi's and a black T-shirt that hugged his muscles.

She cleared her throat. "I was looking for the bathroom."

"It's time to go. Use the one on the plane."

"I hate walking around on planes."

"You're kidding."

Her fear might seem silly to some, but it was quite real to her. "No. I'm not kidding. I hate flying."

His gaze swept her body—a lingering, sizzling inspection—before he brought his eyes back to hers. "I missed you last night."

He had? "Don't say that."

"Why not? It's true."

"We agreed, no personal stuff on the road. It's too dangerous."

The announcement came over the intercom again. "Come on. We have to board."

Amanda reached out and grabbed his arm, stalling him. "We did agree, right, Brad?"

Kurt charged toward them, waving for them to get going. "Damn, people," he spouted. "Get a move on."

"Coming," Amanda said, turning away from Brad and starting forward. He fell into step beside her. Already she was making a spectacle of herself with Brad. Drawing attention where she didn't need it.

She was so in trouble.

BRAD MANAGED TO RESIST Amanda for three hours and fifty-five minutes. That's how long it had been since he'd sworn off her on the plane. Now, sitting in the hotel bar, tables pushed together to accommodate the team, Amanda sat several seats down and across from him. He tried to remember his list of reasons not to do Amanda again. Oh, yeah, his career, his contract, his mother needing him close. All these things meant he couldn't take risks and become headlines.

But just when he'd wrapped his mind around those

concepts, Becker sat next to Amanda, apparently over the cold shoulder he'd been giving her. Brad watched as the kid flirted with her, and tossed gloating looks in Brad's direction. Brad so wanted to ram the fact he'd already won their bet down Becker's throat. The kid was lucky there was an audience and that Brad had promised Amanda not to tell anyone about them.

Tony slapped the table, pulling Brad out of a fantasy where he jacked Becker against a wall and made him cry like a baby. "When Amanda screamed I realized she was locked in the bathroom. I thought I was going to roll out of my seat laughing," Tony said, reaching for his beer.

"Have you ever been in a bathroom when a plane drops half out of the sky?" she demanded. "I was sure my head was going through the ceiling."

"It wasn't as bad as you thought," Reggie told her, biting back laughter unsuccessfully. "Drink up. You're still frazzled."

"I was worried about you," Becker offered, acting sincere.

"I bet you were," Brad said, unable to hold back. "Afraid she wouldn't live long enough to retract that garter story?"

Becker's face colored but he didn't get to respond. Jack, who'd arrived a couple hours after the team, and now sat several seats down from Amanda, took a dig at her.

"Maybe you should sedate her for the next flight," Jack commented. "Might make things more tolerable." He chuckled and brought his beer to his lips, taking a drink. "Nothing more distracting than a screaming female."

Amanda cast him a sticky-sweet smile. "Tell me, Jack. When was the last time you heard a female scream?"

The entire table exploded in laughter. Jack shook his head, smiling. "You are something, Amanda." He paused. "Speaking of making women scream, I arranged a little treat for you gentlemen. A private party down at The Red Zone. Free drinks and hot women. Bring your own dollar bills." Hoots of appreciation flared around the table. When they died down Jack eyed Amanda. "You're welcome to come."

Brad heard Becker offer to stay to keep Amanda company. Amanda declined. Good. The job was taken. Now all Brad had to do was wait for the guys to leave.

Exactly an hour later, he'd ditched the team. After a failed attempt to get her room number from the desk clerk, he called Amanda's cell.

"Brad?" Surprise registered in her voice when she answered.

"What room are you in?"

"What? I can't tell you that."

"Why not?"

"We agreed. No sex. I mean, no contact on the road."

"Define *sex*," he said.

She made a frustrated sound. "Nothing remotely like sex."

He frowned. "All right. We'll order room service and I'll keep my hands to myself."

"No, you won't."

"Okay, no, I won't. Tell me your room number."

"Brad."

God, he loved the way she said his name. "You know you want to."

"You always say that."

He smiled into the phone. "Only because it's true."

"We can't."

"No one will know."

"Another one of your famous lines," she replied. "I figured you'd be out with the guys at the topless bar."

"There's only one woman I want to see topless." He softened his voice. "Please, Amanda. I'm dying here."

"You make me do things I know I shouldn't, Brad Rogers."

"The feeling is mutual, sweetheart. Believe me."

"Room 125," she whispered and hung up.

18

AT 5:00 A.M. THE DAY the team left for Dallas, having completed the Houston series, Amanda stood at her hotel door saying her goodbyes to Brad.

He held her close, his hands sliding beneath her silk robe to touch her naked skin. He should be leaving so that he'd be in his own room before the team was up and about. Instead, he seemed to linger.

"Don't be nervous about the flight." He kissed her nose. "It's a short hop, up and down, and it's over."

They had their plan worked out. They'd take seats far apart from one another on the plane. They'd pretend they weren't intimate with every inch of each other's bodies. They'd pretend they hadn't spent every night of this trip exploring each other with slow, exquisite perfection.

"I hate take off and landing. I'll pretty much be in hell."

"I wish I could sit with you and keep your mind off of it." He nuzzled her neck. "Pull down the shade and shut your eyes. Think about all those things I did to you last night."

"Hmm," she said, smiling. "There's a plan that might actually work."

"You remember I'm meeting your sister later tonight, right? I really appreciate you setting this up."

Her hands settled on his chest. She wondered if this would be the last time she'd touch it, the last time she'd be in his arms. "My sister won't walk around the facts. She'll tell you how it is."

He brushed a wayward strand of hair from her face. "Must run in the family."

"My sister makes me look like an angel. She makes a barracuda look like an angel."

"I like direct and honest, so we should get along well." His eyes softened. "I guess I better go before the guys wake up."

Amanda nodded. "Yeah. Guess so."

They stared at each other. Neither saying a word about tonight. For the first time, Brad didn't promise that the night they'd just shared would be their last. But they also didn't speak of having another night together. Amanda wasn't sure what to think of that.

She watched his mouth descend to hers, anticipation building even as emotions rushed over her. Emotions she didn't completely understand. She touched the rough stubble of his morning beard. She loved how he looked when he woke up. So manly. So rumpled and sexy. When his lips touched hers, she felt her chest tighten. Felt her body melt.

The kiss was slow, full of seduction, full of the spark she'd felt during their lovemaking but never in a simple moment such as this one. This was a kiss not about sex. It was a kiss that spoke of affection and tenderness. Had something already taken root despite their best efforts to stay uninvolved?

Long moments later, Brad seemed reluctant to end the kiss, his lips slowly pulling away. His eyes were so blue, she felt as though she were swimming in heaven. They didn't speak. But she could tell he was reeling from what had just happened as much as she was.

But they couldn't name what was between them. They couldn't allow this to be more than sex. Perhaps, they were both afraid of crossing a line that they could never step back over.

Brad's knuckles skimmed her jaw. Then he left. Amanda hugged herself, feeling the loss of his presence in every ounce of her body. And when she was completely alone, she faced the truth.

She was falling in love with Brad.

"ALL DONE, sugar," Kelli said, walking into the exam room where Brad had just been rolled out of an imaging machine. "Sit up and try to relax."

Brad eased into a sitting position and rolled his shoulders, taking in Amanda's sister as she told the technician who'd helped with the testing he could go home. She had the same smooth skin as Amanda, the same long hair, only hers was light brown with blond highlights. She was taller with a fuller figure.

Kelli oozed an inborn, Marilyn Monroe kind of sexuality. She didn't have to dress the role. Even the simple black skirt and blouse seemed to scream sex. There had been a time when he'd liked this type of woman. Now he preferred the soft, sultry combination of innocence and sensuality that Amanda wore like a second skin.

"I said relax," Kelli commented, hands going to her hips. "If you keep grinding your teeth like that you'll need a dentist as well as a surgeon."

"Surgeon?" Brad's gut tightened.

Kelli's expression showed nothing, though Brad tried

damn hard to read her. "Why don't we go into the other room and look at the pictures together?" she asked.

They headed for the exit when a male voice came from a short distance away. "Hello. Kelli?"

A man appeared in the doorway. Tall and thin, his dark hair was speckled with gray at the sides. The instant he spied Brad, he smiled. "Brad Rogers." He offered his hand. "I'm Bill Wright, Amanda and Kelli's father. I'm a huge fan. It's an honor to meet you."

Accepting his hand, Brad said, "Nice to meet you, sir."

"Just Bill. Nobody calls me sir."

Brad wasn't surprised at the response. Bill Wright had one of those easygoing personalities Brad always found himself drawn to instantly.

"We were about to take a look at Brad's test results," Kelli commented. "I imagine he's pretty eager to see them."

"Oh, of course," Bill said. "I'd love to have a look. Two heads for the price of one." He paused. "If that's okay by you?"

"I'd welcome any extra input I can get," Brad said.

A few moments later, the three of them stood around a computer screen. Kelli punched buttons to take them through a series of images of Brad's arm, shoulder and hand, explaining what she saw and pointing to the certain areas of concern.

The two doctors threw out a few medical terms, talking back and forth a bit. Finally, they concluded they shared the same opinion of Brad's treatment options. Bottom line, Brad needed surgery to correct a problem his surgery had caused.

"I was concerned your UCL might be ruptured but it's not," Kelli said.

"Can I put this off until the end of the season?" Brad asked.

"On a limited rotation with proper care, and checkups, yes." Kelli shook her head. "But I don't like it."

Brad let out a breath he didn't even know he was holding. They still had a shot at the playoffs, and he didn't want to miss them. "Thank God."

"You'll have to tell your coach, son," Bill said. "Your team doc needs to be involved, giving you constant support."

"Because if you don't take care of this right, you could do more damage. Honestly, I wish you'd do the surgery now and be safe. I know I'm wasting my breath saying that. So, think about what you want to do and let me know. I can even meet with your coach if I need to."

Brad nodded, not willing to commit to anything right now.

"I'll run grab you some prescriptions and be right back."

Bill pulled a pen from his pocket and handed it to Brad. "Can I talk you out of an autograph, son?"

Brad laughed. "Amanda told me you'd want one."

"Did she tell you she was supposed to get it for me?" Bill yanked a piece of paper off a nearby table and slid it in front of Brad.

"No," Brad said. "She didn't say that but somehow I can't imagine Amanda asking me for an autograph."

"Why's that?"

"Let's just say, she likes to keep me in my place. Anything that might feed my ego, she wouldn't do."

He chuckled. "She thinks you have a big ego?"

"And that I'm arrogant and cocky."

"Are you?" Bill asked.

"Probably. Amanda seems to smash it right back down, though."

"Learned that from her mother. She can put a hurting on a man's ego in a heartbeat."

They chatted a few more minutes, managing to talk both baseball and cars, clicking like old friends. Brad found this little glimpse into Amanda's life appealed to him and he wished she was by his side. The thought scared him a little. These feelings he had for Amanda didn't fit his career plan.

"Okay," Kelli said, stepping back into the room, prescriptions in hand. "We're all set."

"I'll let you two take care of business," Bill said. "Have Amanda bring you by to see those Mustangs if you get time before you leave town."

"Thanks," Brad said. "I'd like that." He wanted to experience more of life with Amanda. He actually wanted her to be here with him, right now, helping him figure out what to do.

Kelli watched her father depart, shoved a long strand of hair behind her ear, and then went over Brad's instructions and medication.

After she finished, she studied him a moment. "It's clear you and my sister are more than friends. She's a reporter and still you trusted her with knowledge of your injury."

What could he say? "Amanda's easy to trust."

Her eyes narrowed. "Don't hurt my sister."

"I don't plan to."

"Yeah, well, that's what everyone says before they hurt someone. Some careers just don't support relationships."

Brad couldn't resist. "Like an athlete, doctor or pilot?"

"She gave you my list." Her lips pursed. "Interesting."

"Yep," Brad said. "It takes one God complex to spot another."

"Guess it does."

Brad didn't know about a God complex, but certain careers encouraged big egos and self-centered attitudes. Brad realized in that moment, he had some serious decisions to make about himself and Amanda and his career.

AN HOUR AFTER parting ways with Kelli—promising to be in touch soon with his decision about surgery—Brad sat alone in the hotel bar. He was afraid to get on the elevator because he could very well end up in Amanda's room. He'd never felt this drawn to a woman. Never had a woman gotten in his head and refused to leave. That alone was proof she was a distraction his career couldn't afford. He needed focus.

Still, no matter how he tried to convince himself of this fact, he yearned to go to Amanda, to talk to her, to touch her. To be with her.

Instead, he stayed where he was. Risking a scandal had become too dangerous. Amanda was too dangerous. He faced surgery now. The obstacles were bigger than ever. The stakes higher.

Kurt sauntered across the bar and sat on the seat across from Brad. "We're headed to Bone Daddy's to eat. Hot women in Daisy Dukes and killer barbecue. Wanna ride with us?"

Brad considered the offer. Maybe this was what he needed, a reminder that there was life after Amanda.

Pushing to his feet, Brad said, "Let's roll."

19

A WEEK AFTER their return from Dallas, Amanda stood in the press box, watching as Brad took the mound. She assumed he'd had decent news from her sister or he wouldn't be pitching. Of course, she didn't know for sure. She hadn't heard from him. Not a call. Not a visit. Nothing. She hadn't asked Kelli about him when she'd picked up her car and had avoided her sister's prodding and probing about their relationship. At that point, Brad had already started giving her the cold shoulder and Amanda had kept her stupidity over him to herself. She didn't need a lecture from Kelli about how crazy she'd been to fall for someone on the list.

"Nervous about tomorrow?" Reggie asked.

He was referring to her photo shoot for *L.A. Woman.* Apparently, since the interview was first arranged, the editors had taken further interest in her. They now planned to put her on the cover.

"Not so much," Amanda said. "I talked with the editor on the phone for a while and really clicked with her. I felt more comfortable with her than I do with Kevin."

Reggie grunted. "That's not hard to do. So, tell me. Since when do you want to sit in the press box?"

She wasn't sure how to answer that question. The

truth was, she felt out of sorts and needed a change, but she didn't want to say that. "Works for everyone else. I figured I'd see why."

"Since when are you worried about what everyone else is doing?" He didn't give her time to answer, pointing at the field. "Rodriquez is up to bat. Did you see him on that Sports-Beat talk show last night?"

"Yeah, I saw him," Amanda said, watching Brad wind up for his first pitch. "Talking all that junk about hitting off any pitcher in the league. Baseball players. Such a cocky bunch."

The ball flew past the batter, untouched. "Oh, man," Reggie said, eyes wide. "Brad is on tonight. How hard was that?"

Amanda eyed him. "Fast. It was fast. You don't know squat about baseball, do you?"

Reggie grinned. "I usually fake it quite well."

The announcer's voice filled the air. "Pitcher Brad Rogers is firing in the balls tonight. That one registered at one-hundred-and-one miles per hour, folks."

Four innings later, Brad started walking people and Amanda could tell his arm hurt. He'd pitched a great game, but from what she'd seen of him, past and present, his arm had simply given out. The coach sent in Casey to relieve with the scoreboard favoring the Rays. Unless Casey blew it, the Rays would log in another win.

"Looks like they might just make the playoffs." Reggie vocalized what she was thinking.

"And we go back to Dallas again in about three weeks," Amanda commented, thinking it would be her last opportunity to visit with her family for a while.

They didn't say much for the rest of the game,

Reggie appearing to read her need for space. But when the Rays won the game, they cheered together and hugged one another.

Amanda hit the locker room in the rush of reporters. She usually hung back and waited until the crowd thinned out. But not this time. Tonight her emotions over Brad were raw and she needed the security of the mass to protect her.

She made her way through the twenty or so reporters around her, trying to pick an interview victim. Unfortunately, her eyes landed on Tony, who stood buck naked as he dried his back with the towel previously around his waist. All this time and she still hadn't gotten used to the blitz of bare butts.

Tony appeared unaffected by his nakedness, fielding questions from three male reporters, one of whom was Jack. Unwilling to be intimidated by Tony's state of undress, Amanda worked her way into the group, a small tape recorder in her hand.

Chin tilted upward to keep her gaze on target, Amanda asked, "The pitchers walked you tonight, only two home runs from your record. What do you have to say about that?"

Jack stood directly across from her. "It's been asked."

"I'm asking again," Amanda said through clenched teeth.

Apparently, Tony didn't mind answering and he launched into a five-minute rant. Take that, Jack Ass. When Tony finally calmed, Amanda moved on, searching for her next victim. She locked gazes with Brad, who stood far too close.

For several seconds, Amanda froze, mesmerized by the man who'd gotten under her skin and refused to leave. The activity around them slipped into the distance and she searched his gaze for answers on why he'd suddenly gone cold. He gave her nothing in that look. Nothing to hint at what he felt. And, lord help her, as much as she'd hoped to snub Brad, she felt his attention in every inch of her body. If only she had an On-Off button.

Someone asked Brad a question and he gave the reporter his focus. Amanda forced herself to scan the rest of the room for another interview.

She decided to talk to Casey, always an easy mark for conversation. "You see the follow-up interview Jack did with me?" he asked.

"I did," Amanda said. "Good stuff."

He lowered his voice, his tone flirtatious. "I'd like a real interview with you. One without references to Brad and garters. Something more personal. Just about me."

"Soon," she said, regretting her choice to chat with him. She wasn't up to his flirtation and games.

"Tonight," he said. "I'll buy you a drink at the after party."

She was going to make the briefest of appearances at the party, get what she needed, and be gone. "Not that soon." When he appeared ready to argue, she added, "Soon, though. I promise. I'll make the garter thing up to you. Let me think of an angle that will really make you shine and we'll set it up." She pretended to wave at someone behind him. "I need to run." She darted away.

Player after player, Amanda worked the room, determined to finish her job before the crowd cleared and she ended up in an awkward situation with Brad. She couldn't avoid him forever, but she sure could tonight.

Amanda waited until four reporters surrounded him

and approached. Questions flowed one after another while she remained silent. Everything that came to Amanda's mind seemed like a betrayal of a confidence she had with Brad. Then a reporter asked Brad the same question she would have, if this had been anyone but Brad. "Can we expect you back with the Rays next year?"

"Right now, expect me on the mound. I can't tell you what colors I'll be wearing."

Amanda knew in that moment she had a job to do. She couldn't hold back because she'd slept with Brad. She cleared her throat and decided to go for it. "When can we expect to know?"

His attention zeroed in on Amanda, his tone sharp. "Right after I know."

"Who are your top prospects?" another reporter asked, following her lead.

"That's not something I'm willing to discuss just yet." He let his gaze travel from the person he was addressing back to Amanda. "But what I can tell you is this. I'm focused on my career. Dedicated and ready to be a leader wherever I play."

She knew he was talking to her, telling her what he didn't have the balls to tell her in private. He had to focus on his career, not her. Amanda smiled and she made sure it was big one. "Well," she said, "that's good news to those of us who prefer the idea of seeing you *on* the field rather than *off.*"

Shock registered on his handsome face. She'd scored her own point. No way was she letting this too-confident and cowardly man know what he meant to her. She stood her ground for the other questions, enjoying the discomfort she sensed in him.

She had a job to do, a dream of her own to achieve. Brad Rogers was not going to stop her. She wasn't giving up anything over a pitcher who just happened to know her strike zone.

20

THREE WEEKS LATER, they were back in Dallas for the first round of playoffs. Amanda walked into the café of the hotel where she and the team were staying, preparing to face the firing squad called her sister. She'd been avoiding Kelli for two days now.

It wasn't that she didn't want to see Kelli. It was more that she didn't want to deal with the emotions that would surface when she was with Kelli. Her sister had a way of seeing through her toughest shell. And right now, Amanda needed to maintain the thick wall she'd erected.

Knowing Kelli would be checking out her attire, Amanda had selected her outfit carefully. She went with a pair of casual Ralph Lauren navy pants and a matching shell with a sporty half-sleeve jacket. And, of course, she wore heels. Navy with white trim.

Amanda had barely hit the door of the restaurant when she heard her name called out. Searching for the source, she found Kurt sitting at a table of about ten players. Brad sat beside him. Amanda raised a hand, intending to go on her own way, but Kurt motioned her forward.

She couldn't avoid Brad forever and the very fact that she wanted to made her mad at herself. Nevertheless, she stopped on the same side of the table as him rather than facing him head-on. She could feel his eyes on her.

Tony patted a chair beside him. "Come on over to my sweet spot, darlin'." Tony had been quite amused over her sweet spot headline and he used every opportunity to use the phrase in conversation.

"As tempting as that offer is, Tony," she said, "I'm meeting my sister for breakfast."

"We can pull up another chair," Kurt suggested. He stood and grabbed a chair, positioning it opposite Brad and next to an available seat. "Sorry, Tony. The ladies are with me."

Amanda stiffened her spine and decided to work through her discomfort. She refused to let Brad mess with her head. Besides, this was a sign of acceptance. The team seemed to be allowing her into their inner circle.

She sat. "I'm warning you guys. My sister is going to work you over."

The guys laughed and made boastful comments about their ability to handle any woman. Amanda smiled to herself. They had no idea what they were up against with Kelli. As if on cue, Kelli appeared at the door. Amanda acknowledged her with the lift of her hand.

Kelli waved back and made her way over. Dressed in a red halter-style dress, Kelli looked casual, sexy and confident. Several whistles sounded around the table, and Amanda rolled her eyes.

She stood and hugged her sister. Then, Kelli assessed the table of men. "Well, hello, gentlemen." Murmured replies followed as she sat and smiled at both Kurt and Brad. "Great game last night."

"I take it you like baseball?" Kurt asked.

"I like baseball players," she said.

"Kelli's a sports medicine doctor. She treats a lot of baseball players," Amanda said.

"I take good care of my players." Kelli eyed Kurt with a flirtatious smile. "I happen to know a few members of your competition quite well."

Kurt laughed at that. "Do you, now?"

"I know their weak spots," Kelli added, then took a sip of her water. "Of course, that's privileged information. You'll have to beat the Rangers all by yourselves." She turned to Amanda. "I have a surprise." She reached her oversize purse and removed a copy of *L.A. Woman*.

"How did you get this?" Amanda asked, accepting the magazine. "Is it even on shelves yet?"

"Tomorrow. I pulled a few strings to get it early. You look gorgeous, by the way, and the story inside is great." Kelli winked. "Daddy wants you to autograph it for him."

Amanda glanced up in time to catch a hint of a smile on Brad's face. She knew from Kelli that her father had hit up Brad for his autograph. Apparently they'd gotten along well. Hearing that from Brad would have been nice.

"Are you going to show us or what?" Kurt asked.

Amanda passed the magazine around. She hadn't told anyone, but *L.A. Woman* had offered her a job. She'd declined, thinking the newspaper was where she wanted to be. But seeing the magazine, and given the awkwardness she'd felt during this trip, not to mention the constant pressure to achieve from Kevin despite her successes, she wasn't so sure that it had been the right choice.

The magazine was handed to Brad. He stared at the

cover a moment before his eyes lifted to Amanda's. "Congratulations."

Their gazes held for several seconds. She wanted so badly to understand what was going on with him, with them. "Thank you," she said.

Somehow, she managed to smile and converse through breakfast, acting as though Brad was just another ballplayer. The facade lasted until she walked her sister to her car.

"What is going on with you and Brad?" Kelli demanded the minute they were alone.

"Nothing. Nothing is going on."

"Amanda, this is me you're talking to. Your sister, who knows you like she knows herself. The awkwardness between the two of you was thick enough to have its own chair. I got the impression you two were a hot item when he was at my office. And so did Dad."

What could Amanda say? "Well, we're not."

Kelli reached over to push hair out of Amanda's eyes. "What happened, sweetie?"

"Nothing." Amanda tried to laugh, but the sound came out sort of choked. "We had a quick, hot—really hot—roll in the sheets. I made a stupid mistake that could have ruined my career."

"Ah, sweetie. You fell hard, didn't you?"

Amanda nodded, confessing to the only person in the world she dared. "I'm such a fool. You warned me off ballplayers."

"No. Not a fool. We don't always have a choice over who we fall for. Our hearts do the picking. How does Brad feel about you?"

"We're over, so it's irrelevant. I just want to forget about it all now."

"He trusted you with his injury. I know pro athletes and that's big."

"I suppose." She shrugged. "I've been around you and Daddy enough to spot an injured player. I guessed."

"You didn't have proof. He could have denied he was hurt."

"I slept with him, Kelli. I didn't want anyone to know. He doesn't want anyone to know about his arm. We have dirty little secrets neither wants spread. That's not trust. It's blackmail."

Kelli opened her mouth and shut it again, seeming to reconsider what she'd been about to say. "If you need to talk, you know where I am."

"I do." Amanda hugged her.

Right now, though, she didn't want to talk. She didn't even want to think about Brad. She wanted to put him behind her.

Besides, she'd come up with an idea on what to do with the steroid story. She was interviewing Casey later today and he'd agreed to give her a candid interview about the pressure of going from the minors to the majors. If she couldn't beat Jack to the steroid story, she could be the one to bring up the forbidden topic first. She was going to ask Casey about the things he'd seen, no names required. She'd do this story in a way that promoted a drug-free sport.

And if that didn't make Kevin happy, Amanda had to start accepting that she might not be the right person for this job.

LATE IN THE AFTERNOON of the team's final day in Dallas, Brad sauntered into the hotel after his acupuncture appointment. He'd be pitching tonight and he wanted to be at his best, especially with the encouraging news he'd gotten from his agent earlier. Mike reported several conversations in progress regarding Brad's contract. None of them were with the Rays, but Mike planned to let the team owner know there was competitive interest in Brad, with the intention to apply pressure to re-sign him. It was a relief that teams were seeking him because all the pressure to perform, coupled with all the secrets, was wearing on him.

He spotted Kurt in the sports bar to his right. Or rather heard him. Kurt was talking loudly, pointing at the television and laughing with the bartender.

Brad walked over, noting one of the playoff games was the focus of attention. No wonder Kurt was being rowdy. A few steps inside the bar, Brad stopped in his tracks. In the back corner booth, Amanda was sitting with Becker. Alone.

Everything inside him went cold. Seeing Amanda, wanting her, but not touching her, had been one of the hardest feats he'd ever accomplished. Seeing her in that booth, cozy with Becker, damn near tore Brad up inside. The urge to charge forward and claim what was his overwhelmed him.

But she wasn't his. The sound of snapping fingers drew his attention to Kurt, who motioned Brad over. Suddenly, he realized he was standing in the middle of the bar making a total ass of himself staring at Amanda.

He scrubbed his jaw as he sat on the bar stool next to Kurt. "They've been here about an hour," Kurt said, without being asked, his voice low, his tone serious.

"I didn't ask," Brad said, grabbing a peanut from the bowl in front of him and cracking the shell because he needed to do something with the tension threatening to overwhelm him.

"But you wanted to know," Kurt said. "We both know you wanted to."

Brad tossed the shell on the bar. "I decided weeks ago to tune out Becker. I've got more important things to worry about than him or some stupid bet."

"I see," Kurt said. "More important than Amanda, too, I guess. You know, sitting on the sideline, as I'm doing, gives a clear perspective. If you don't get your head out of your ass real fast, she's going to be gone."

Brad's gut tightened. He knew Kurt was right. He also knew that if he went to Amanda again, there would be no backing out. No question about it. The next go round would be for keeps.

He needed to work this out in his own time, though. He couldn't talk with Kurt about it, even as much as he trusted him.

"Mike has contract talks rolling," Brad said, changing the subject to one he could discuss with Kurt. "Not with the Rays, but he feels that's coming soon."

"So why don't you seem happy?"

"I need surgery on my arm again." Brad went on to explain the details. "So, here is the dilemma. How can I sign a new contract and not tell them about my arm? For a long time I thought that I'd come back from the last surgery too soon and that once I'd rested, I'd be good. Now, I know better."

"It's freaking amazing how well you've pitched through this," Kurt said.

"Acupuncture, man. Amanda's sister has me hooked for life."

"The fact that Amanda knows about all of this says

a lot," Kurt commented. "I know. Bad subject." He held up a hand to forestall whatever Brad might have said.

Kurt drummed his fingers on the bar. "You're right, you know," he said. "It's a dilemma. I mean, let's face it. They treat us like commodities. It's about money and performance. Nothing else."

"That's exactly what management is all about. Greedy bastards."

"And that's who you're dealing with here. Part of me says, screw it, don't say a word until after the deal's done and then they'll have to cope. Especially since you're feeling the prognosis is good, and your pitching is damn good right now." He sighed. "But then there's the other part of me—the part that still hears my mama's lectures about doing what's right—that says, speak up."

Brad took it all in, thankful he'd talked to Kurt. Just telling someone felt good.

It had felt good telling Amanda, too. Having her to share his struggles had given him a boost and helped his perspective. But she was gone now. Without consciously doing so, Brad looked toward her table, hoping for a glimpse of one of her smiles. Unfortunately, Becker looked up at that moment. The kid smiled and waved, a satisfied expression on his face. Damn it, right now the kid had everything he wanted. Becker had his whole career in front of him and he had Amanda by his side.

Brad sat back, startled by that thought. He realized the truth that had been nudging at him. He wanted—no, needed—more than another five years in the game. He needed Amanda by his side for the ride.

Not sure what to do with this new information, he pushed to his feet and gave Kurt a nod. "Check you later, man."

Brad needed some time alone to think.

21

AMANDA WOKE UP one morning groggy and disoriented. Where was she? Right. Chicago. Second round of the playoffs. She stumbled to her hotel room door and grabbed the paper that had been slid underneath. She plopped down on the bed and reached for the phone, intent on ordering coffee. But the front page of the entertainment section distracted her before she could place her order. There was a huge picture of Tony with a woman hanging all over him.

"Hello?"

Amanda realized she was still holding the phone. "Oh. Yes. Hello. I mean, I'll call back."

She dropped the receiver on the base and pressed her hand to her forehead. Jack's conversation with Laura in the L.A. airport rushed through Amanda's mind. He'd set Tony up. She bet a million bucks he was behind those photos. He'd been out partying with the guys almost nightly, so he'd had plenty of opportunity. And he'd promised Laura he would prove Tony was no good.

Jack's ambition knew no boundaries if he'd go to these lengths to convince Laura to confide in him. And Amanda could do nothing to ward off this disaster. Relations between her and Laura had been strained ever since she'd suggested Laura dump Tony and find someone else. Why hadn't Amanda kept her mouth shut? She could have put up with Laura's obsessing.

I did this, she thought, as she grabbed the phone and asked for Tony's room. Her recent story about the steroids issue had hit the stands, no doubt applying performance pressure on Jack. Kevin had been on top of the world, since his source claimed Jack was feeling the heat.

After several rings a sleepy-sounding Tony answered.

"Tony. It's Amanda. What room are you in?"

"1050. Why?"

"We need to talk."

"I'm asleep," he complained.

"Grab today's paper and check out the entertainment page. You need to see me. I'll be there in twenty minutes."

Exactly twenty minutes later, Amanda was knocking on Tony's door. She'd tossed on some clothes and done the minimum to look presentable. Before leaving her room she'd tried phoning Laura's cell but had only gotten through to voice mail.

No answer. A door farther down the hallway opened and Brad appeared. Amanda's heart fell to her feet. He stared and blinked, as if he thought he was seeing a ghost.

Finally, Tony answered and Amanda moved forward, eager to avoid Brad. Days had passed since they'd spoken, and now was not the time to get reunited.

The minute Amanda entered the hotel room Tony started to rant in a mix of Italian and English. He wore jeans and nothing else. "I'm screwed. Laura—"

Amanda's gaze went to the bed, where a woman lay naked but for a well-placed sheet. She waved at Amanda.

"Holy shit, Tony!" Amanda cut her hands in the air. "Why is she here?"

"She doesn't have a ride."

"Get her a cab."

"Hey," the woman protested. "Who do you think you are?"

Amanda answered the woman but spoke to Tony. "I'm the one who can save your ass. Meet me in the café downstairs in five minutes." She paused. "Alone."

Before Amanda could leave a knock sounded on the door. "Great. Just what we need. More company."

Tony frowned and moved to the door. "Who is it?"

"It's Brad, Tony. Let me in."

Tony yanked open the door before Amanda could say anything. Wasn't this a cozy ensemble—a naked woman, an angry Italian and the man who knew all of her sweet spots but no longer wanted to use them. This was hell.

Brad stepped toward Amanda, his expression grim. "What are you doing in Tony's room?"

"What business is it of yours, Brad?" she demanded, furious he had the gall to question her when he'd ignored her for all this time.

"I happen to know how important your job is to you. Do you know how this looks?"

Amanda let out a bark of harsh laughter. "You found us out, Brad. Me, Tony and Alice have a hot thing going on."

"My name isn't Alice."

"Sweetheart, I don't care what your name is," Amanda said.

Brad swore. "What the hell, Amanda?"

"Don't curse at me!"

"I don't know what this is all about and frankly, I don't care." Tony raised his voice. "I'm having a freaking crisis here. Can we get back to me?"

Amanda glared at Tony. "Meet me in the café in an hour."

"I thought you said five minutes. I need to talk now."

"I changed my mind. I'm going to take a shower and call Laura. I suggest you do a little housecleaning."

Tony seemed as though he wanted to argue but refrained. "Fine."

Brad grabbed Amanda's arm as she turned to leave. "Amanda."

"Let go."

He did as she requested, but was on her heels when she stepped into the hallway. She started for the elevator when he attempted to redirect her toward his room.

She dug in her heels. "No."

The elevator opened and a room service attendant stepped out. Brad glanced at the man and let go of Amanda. She darted away, but he followed her into the elevator. She hit the lobby level, afraid to go to her room because of what she might do if alone with Brad.

Silence filled the car.

"I missed you," he said softly.

She didn't look at him. Didn't dare. "You have a funny way of showing it."

"We need to talk."

Not a chance.

She whirled around to face him. "We had a fling. It's over. End of subject. Or it would have been if you hadn't blasted your way into Tony's room. How do you suggest we explain your territorial he-man routine? Because you just royally screwed me." She paused. "Again."

His face flashed with surprise as the doors opened. Amanda rushed forward, desperate to get away from him. She managed all of a few steps before Brad crowded her with his larger body, dictating where she went. She could either go along with him or bring attention to herself, a fact he no doubt counted on. Suddenly, Brad yanked her into a tiny handicapped bathroom.

"What do you think you are doing?" she demanded as he locked the door.

In one swift move, he picked her up, set her on top of the counter, and pressed her legs apart. He stepped between them as if he had that right. "Do you know how furious I was when I saw you go into Tony's room?"

She wasn't a toy to be played with. "You have no say over what I do or who I do it with."

"What if I said I want to? What if I said I care about everything you do?"

She felt her lips tremble despite her efforts to act unaffected. "I'd say you have a funny way of showing it. Not that it matters. I can't keep doing this with you, Brad. I can't."

He tilted his head forward and inhaled. "I love how you smell."

Amanda's hands curled against the counter to keep from touching him. She didn't want to fall under his spell again.

"No more, Brad."

Their eyes locked and his burned with heat. His thumbs slid back and forth on her cheeks, the callused tips sending a rush of sensation through her entire body. "I missed you, Amanda."

She wanted to believe him but she didn't dare.

When she didn't respond, he added, "Tell me you missed me, too,"

"We both know we can't do this."

"We can."

Amanda squeezed her eyes shut. "No." The word was barely audible.

His lips hovered above hers, his breath warm and tantalizing as he responded. "Yes." His mouth brushed hers. "Yes."

Then they were kissing. A slow, sensual slide of tongues that seduced, taking Amanda beyond reason. In only a few moments, the gentle, sensual kiss transformed into something hot and wildly passionate. Brad's hands were everywhere, molding her to him, as she wrapped her legs around his waist. His touch, his mouth, his body, demanded her participation and she gave it freely, no longer willing to fight. No man set her on fire this way.

His palms skimmed her skirt upward, caressing her bare legs. While their tongues tangled, tasted, devoured, his fingers eased past her silk thong.

She gasped as he slid two fingers along her sensitive flesh, spreading the proof of her arousal and teasing her clit with excruciating perfection. Instinct and need pressed her onward, and Amanda reached for his pants, releasing his erection and circling the width with her hand, guiding him to where she ached for completion. Moments later, he was inside her, filling her, completing her in a way she didn't remember sex ever doing.

Brad tore his mouth from hers and for several seconds their eyes locked. The connection to him she felt shook her to the core. And when he slowly lowered his head to claim her mouth again, she melted, lost in the stroke of his tongue, in the feel of his hard body buried deep in hers, seducing her with ease. With perfection.

Somehow, her shirt was gone, tossed aside, the front clasp of her bra unlatched. Brad's hands were on her breasts, molding and kneading, his teeth nipping her bottom lip, tongue following the action, soothing.

"You drive me insane with need," he murmured before kissing her again, his cock doing a slow sensual slide back and forth, his fingers plucking at her nipples.

He pressed her hands to her breasts. "Touch yourself like I was," he said, straightening, hands going to her hips, anchoring her as he began to pump.

She did as he said, filling her hands with her breasts, aroused by the heat in his eyes as she teased her nipples. Aroused as she watched the flex of muscle in his powerful arms, wishing he was naked. She wanted him naked.

She reached for his shirt, moving her hands beneath the material. She clung to him anywhere, everywhere, never managing to get his shirt off. Never managing to get enough of him. Of his touch, his mouth, his hands.

Her hips rocked against his, the rise of release starting to rush through her body. "Brad. I am…" But the words were gone as she felt the first ripple of orgasm expand. Her muscles grab his cock, pulling him deeper, taking him in. When he pulled back, preparing to thrust, she wanted to scream for his return. And when he dove deep, burying himself to the hilt, shaking with his own release, she sighed with the final, perfect spasms of orgasm.

Long moments later, he lifted his head from where he'd rested it on her shoulder and brushed his lips over hers, tenderness in his expression. Amanda's chest tightened with the emotion she felt. She loved him.

And that scared the hell out of her.

Carefully, Brad eased her legs down, her feet to the ground. Feeling awkward, uncertain of what came next, or even what she expected or wanted, Amanda gave him her back. She dressed quickly, quiet anticipation charging the air.

When Amanda completed her task, Brad embraced her. "Amanda—"

Her cell phone rang and she said a silent thank-you. She was afraid to hear what he had to say. "It could be Laura. I have to take it." She reached for her purse sitting in the center of the sink and pulled out her cell.

Amanda answered. "Laura. Hi. Hold on." She covered the phone, and spoke to Brad. "I have to get out of here."

"We need to talk."

No, they didn't. "Not here. Not now."

"We're going to talk, Amanda. Soon. Have no doubt. I'll wait for you in the café." He disappeared out the door.

Amanda let out a breath and then took the call. "Hi, Laura. Thanks for calling me back."

No tears this time. "You saw the paper, I guess?" Laura asked. Her voice was tight. "I'm going to make that sorry jerk pay. I'm going to tell the world his secrets and then he can kiss his career goodbye."

Exactly what Amanda expected. "What secret, Laura?"

"Steroids," she said. "That's how he gets all those great hits. He's juicing. I know you wanted the story and I'm sorry. Jack called and told me about the paper and I was pretty upset. I told him everything. I can tell you, too. The more bad press Tony gets, the better."

Telling Laura Jack had set up Tony wasn't likely to help. "Do you have proof, Laura?"

"I saw him inject himself. If they test him, they'll know."

"How do you know it was steroids?"

"What else would it be?"

Amanda went down a short list of possible things, including vitamin supplements.

"Well, it's not any of those things," Laura said, rejecting Amanda's suggestions. "It's steroids. Test him."

"You don't know any of this with certainty and you're putting the man's career on the line."

"He should have thought of that before he did what he did."

"The entire team is affected by this kind of scandal, Laura. They're in the playoffs. They need Tony on the field."

"I guess the team will find out what a jerk he is, too."

Several minutes later, Amanda hung up the phone, having gotten nowhere except frustrated with Laura. She leaned on the bathroom sink, surveying her image in the mirror and noting her swollen lips.

Why had she let that happen with Brad? Why? She couldn't think about that now. She had to think about Tony. And though she didn't agree with Tony doing steroids—if he really was—she understood the desperate need to stay competitive.

This new career of hers had placed her in a horrible position. She hated the idea of destroying someone for a story. How had her job become that? Jack Krass, Tony, Laura. The battle to get the story first, no matter who was destroyed. This wasn't her way. But before she could even think about that big issue, she had to deal with the current crisis.

22

"SHE TALKED to Laura?" Tony asked. He sat across from Brad in the café.

Brad regarded Tony, thinking about how furious he'd been when he'd seen Amanda entering his room. "Yeah. She talked to her. I have no idea of the outcome, though."

"Where is she?" Tony asked, his tone impatient.

"She'll be here."

Tony drummed his fingers on the table and waved away a waitress. "What's up with you two?"

"Nothing. And that's the story I expect you to stick to."

"Just asking, man. Trust me, I won't be running my mouth. Amanda's the last person I want to piss off right now." He narrowed his eyes on Brad. "But I have to say. I've never seen you act so nuts over a woman."

Brad could well imagine his behavior had taken Tony off guard. Hell, his lack of control took him off guard, too. His gaze went to the doorway, feeling the familiar punch of excitement in his gut at the sight of her. "She's here."

He watched her approach, noting the apprehension in her face. He wished he wasn't partly responsible for it.

Amanda sat between him and Tony. One of her perfect ivory cheeks had been rubbed red from his stubble.

Sensual images of being buried deep inside her, the warm, wet heat of her body surrounding him, played in his mind. Primitive, possessive feelings rushed over him.

He'd fallen in love with Amanda.

What else could explain the way his heart beat faster every time she was near? Or the way he felt calmer, happier, more complete, when he was with her.

Man, did his timing suck.

"Unfortunately, Jack got to Laura before I did. Frankly, I think he set you up. I heard him at the airport, talking to Laura, promising he'd prove you were a jerk. Laura said Jack called her this morning to tell her about the picture, otherwise she wouldn't have known."

"That sorry bastard." Tony ground out the words between his teeth. "He's the one who invited us to the club where that picture was taken. I didn't think anything about it. He's always inviting us places. But come to think about it, that night he hung by my side a lot. Every time I turned around, he was there."

"The details of how we got here aren't that important right now," Brad commented. "The damage is done. How bad is the damage?"

Amanda exhaled. "First, let me say this, Tony. I'm not accusing you of anything. I'm only repeating what I've been told."

"Just tell me."

"Laura says you're taking steroids and she gave Jack the details. She says she witnessed you inject yourself."

Tony stared at Amanda, his expression blank. He didn't say a word.

That was a bad sign, Brad thought. "It's just her word against his, right?" he asked. "Or is there more?"

"It's enough to raise concerns and taint Tony's

image," Amanda noted. "Jack isn't a fool. He'll make sure he doesn't say with certainty that Tony is juicing. He'll buzz the possibility."

"Which will ruin me," Tony said quietly. "Guilty or innocent, people won't look at me the same."

"Are you guilty?" Brad asked.

Tony looked at Amanda and Brad knew he was nervous about talking in front of her. "You can trust her," Brad said. "It's off the record. Right Amanda?"

"Absolutely."

Tony appeared skeptical. Brad figured the best way to convince Tony was to confess his own secret. "I'm injured and I've been hiding it. Amanda's known all along. Obviously, she hasn't turned me into a headline.

"I need surgery. Good news is I can work through the playoffs. But between the injury and all the bad press this past year, my contract renewal is up in the air. I'm praying my performance is good enough to convince management to re-sign me. Either way, I'm tired of hiding."

Brad focused on Amanda with those final words, hoping she'd read the double meaning. There had to be a way they could be together without compromising their careers.

Of course, if she was his wife, no one could protest. *His wife.* What a crazy thought. But he actually contemplated the idea. He may have known her only a short time, but he couldn't imagine another day without her.

Tony cleared his throat, drawing the attention back to him. "I'm clean."

Amanda gave him a probing stare, as if she didn't quite believe him. "Why is Laura so sure you aren't?"

"Off the record." He waited for her nod before continuing. "I'm clean *now*. There was a time when I couldn't say that."

Brad cursed. "Damn it, Tony. You know what I think of that shit."

"Well, Brad, not everyone is as confident as you. Not everyone can be a star without a little help."

"Man, in case you forgot, I've been dodging my walking papers for a year. You just heard me admit I've been hiding an injury. Confidence damn sure wasn't my motivation. The pressure gets to all of us."

"You're injured and you still manage to throw hundred-mile-an-hour balls when other guys never break three digits," Tony stated, his words almost accusing. "Don't judge me, man. You're not like me. You didn't struggle to get here. We both know you were a star from Little League to the pros. I didn't even get off the bench until my senior year in college. But I told you. I'm done with that shit. I'm clean."

Brad's path hadn't been as easy as Tony thought, but there was no point in saying so.

"Willing to take a test and prove you're clean?" she asked.

Tony didn't hesitate. "Yeah. I'll test."

"Good," she said. "I suggest we go to your coach today because Jack will act immediately. Get tested. Tomorrow morning I'll print the story along with a copy of the negative results, provided we get approval from everyone involved to print them. That will shut down any and all doubt. Tomorrow isn't my feature day but I'm sure my boss will clear some space for this."

Brad ran his hand over his jaw. "Have him clear double. Might as well spill my news at the same time."

He turned to Tony. "I'm glad you're clean. I know using must be tempting when you're so close to a record."

"You have no idea," Tony murmured, almost as if he were speaking to himself. "I just want this to go away."

"We'll make it go away," Amanda assured him. "I need to shower and change. One of you want to call me once you've talked to the coach?"

"I'll call Coach," Brad said. "And I'll let you know the time."

She pushed to her feet. "See you both soon."

"Amanda," Tony said, his voice low but intense.

She faced him. "Yes?"

"Thank you."

Her expression was serious. "Thank me by getting that record at tomorrow's game."

Tony grinned. "You have my word." .

THIRTY MINUTES AFTER her meeting with Brad and Tony, Amanda stepped into the shower. The hot water streamed over her face, and now that she was alone, she could process all that she'd been through this morning.

At some point she'd lost her room key, which necessitated an ordeal at the front desk to get a replacement. She'd barely walked through her door when she'd received a call from *L.A. Woman* again offering her a job. This time with added incentives. Apparently, their feature on Amanda had generated tons of response from readers.

The new incentives included the freedom to write about whatever she wanted as long as the subject appealed to their readers. Sports were fine, but that would not be her exclusive focus. However, they did want her to host an online sports blog. She'd be free to spread her wings and make her features unique, and she'd be able to work from home. The kicker was a substantial increase in pay.

She'd be crazy not to take it.

Amanda had asked for a few days to consider the offer, thankful they'd been willing to wait. Of course, she should take the job. No more Jack Ass. No more careers to ruin for the sake of a story. No more facing Brad. So why was she hesitating?

Leaning forward, Amanda allowed the warm water to pour over her head, neck and shoulders. She squeezed her eyes shut against the images in her mind. Images of showering with Brad, of his hands turning her inside out with need.

The curtain moved behind her. "Amanda."

Amanda's eyes went wide as Brad joined her. "How'd you get in here?"

"I knocked and you didn't answer."

"That still doesn't explain how you got in here."

"You dropped your key and I grabbed it. I kind of hoped it was an invitation."

"I didn't even know I dropped it."

"Do you want me to leave?"

Amanda blinked, unable to find words. Lord help her, she knew she should tell him to leave before he frazzled her emotions any more than he already had. But she couldn't seem to muster the will to send him away.

"No," she whispered. "I don't want you to leave."

Before she even finished her sentence, Brad's strong arms surrounded her. "I'm sorry for the way I've acted. Forgive me."

Her palms settled on the width of his chest. "You don't owe me an apology. We promised each other nothing."

"Let's change that," he said. "Take a shower with me every day, Amanda."

"What?" Amanda could hardly breathe as the fear of being hurt took hold. She shook her head. "Don't say things like that."

His hands framed her face. "Take a shower with me every day. I know your job complicates things, but somehow we'll figure it out. I need you, Amanda. Like I've never needed anyone."

She could barely believe she was hearing this. She stared into his eyes and found sincerity. Everything inside her warmed and emotions forced themselves to the surface. "I want to believe you."

"I'll show you how much. No matter how long it takes, Amanda. I'll show you."

His mouth came down on hers, kissing her with passion. Amanda leaned into him, not willing to think about the future, or even the past. Only this moment.

He whispered her name and then deepened the kiss. The long, hard length of his arousal settled between her legs. Brad lifted her, hands around her backside, positioning her against the far wall. When he set her back down, he held on to one of her legs, wrapping it around his hip. He kissed her as he slid into her willing body, sinking deep. He braced one hand on the wall above her head, anchoring them as they started to move together. This wasn't the wild passion they'd often experienced. This was slow, sensual lovemaking.

Their hips rocked in unison, a tantalizing dance matching the long, hot strokes of their tongues. She explored every inch of his delicious torso. Beneath her palms he flexed, taut skin over sexy muscle. She couldn't get enough of him and pressed her body tight to his, her nipples nestled in the soft hair of his chest. If she could have climbed under his skin, she would have.

He responded to her silent demands, settling his hands on her backside, and angled her hips to take him deeper and deeper. She gasped with the heavy strokes of his cock teasing the sweetest of places. Her actions begged for more, begged him not to stop.

Murmuring his name, she kissed his shoulder, his neck. She buried her face there, clinging to him as he responded to her with a hard thrust. And another. Over and over he pumped his cock into her, taking and giving. Giving and taking.

And then, without warning, Amanda exploded. No slow build. No suggestion of what was to come. Just a sudden wave of spasms delivering jolts of pleasure so intense they rendered her paralyzed. Distantly, she heard him say her name, felt him shudder, and knew he, too, had found satisfaction.

They clung to one another, bodies sated and wet. It was as if they both feared that by speaking, the moment would end.

Brad rested his forehead to hers. "I've never had a woman do what you do to me. I want you in my life, Amanda. We can find a way around our challenges. Tell me you want that."

There was no place for logic in her response. There was only the answer in her heart. "I do."

HOURS LATER, Amanda sat behind the desk in her room typing her story about Tony. Her boss was waiting eagerly for the finished product. She wore shorts and a tank top, feeling comfortable and happy. Wearing only his boxers,

Brad lay across the bed, ice pack on his arm as he watched ESPN. Like her father, Brad could watch sports nonstop. Good thing she could, too. She smiled as he mumbled about a bad call some umpire had made. Having him here, simply hanging out with her, felt wonderful.

She still couldn't believe he'd shown up in her shower. Nor could she believe how happy she was. How fulfilled. They were taking a flight home to L.A. together, separate from the team. That would allow them to discuss how to get through all their complications.

Brad pushed off the bed, dropping his ice pack in the bucket on the nightstand and walked behind her. He settled his hands on her shoulders, gently kneading her tense muscles. "How's it going?"

She punched a final key to send the story to Kevin and swiveled around in her chair, holding on to one of Brad's hands as she smiled up at him. "All done. With Tony's story, at least. Your story will run a few days from now so I'm not rushed on it."

He tugged her to her feet and into his arms. "If I wear a disguise, will you sneak into a movie with me?"

She smiled. The idea of sneaking into a movie sounded wonderful. Maybe one day they wouldn't have to sneak. "Only if that offer includes a giant popcorn."

"I'll get you two giant popcorns if it'll get me a movie date."

She laughed. "You're on."

His gaze swept her face, admiration washing over his features. "You were great with Coach. You earned a lot of trust today, Amanda. Do you really think people will judge you for being with me?"

She knew she'd made progress today but not enough

to change the perceptions female reporters battled in the industry. If only it could be different. "Of course, they will. Jack will say you're the reason I got these stories."

"Mike Martin from the Sox is married to a female reporter."

"Good thing she's female."

"Always a smart-ass." He played with a loose strand of her hair. "My point is that their relationship is accepted."

But she and Brad weren't married. And she felt awkward mentioning that. The depth of what she felt for him in such a short time scared the hell out of her. So much so, she suddenly needed a bit of space, uncomfortable with how transparent this conversation might make her.

Amanda tried to push out of Brad's arms but he held her steady. "Whoa. What's wrong?"

She stared at his chest. "Our circumstances are different. *L.A. Woman* offered me a job. I might take it."

"But then you wouldn't travel with the team."

"No, but I'd work from home and have the freedom to cover any story I wanted to."

"You wouldn't have an excuse to be around the team."

"We wouldn't have to hide." She went on to explain the offer in more detail.

When she'd finished, Brad studied her several seconds. "We'll work things out no matter which job you choose. Promise me you'll base the decision on what you want, not on what you think best suits our relationship. This is your dream. I have mine. We'll work out the rest."

"Brad—"

"Promise me. We will find a way to be together no matter what."

Amanda didn't know what to say. She'd never been with a man who didn't put his needs first. That Brad worried over her career mattered more than she could find the words to say. "Thank you, Brad."

"For what?"

"For caring."

"Don't thank me for that because I can't help myself." He pulled her close, his chin settling on her head. "Ah, baby, you don't get it yet. But you will. I'm going to make sure you do."

23

THE LAST-MINUTE press conference inside the airport was winding down. Amanda, Jack, Tony and his coach had fielded questions from about forty reporters and cameramen. Amanda was often pitted against Jack, questioned about their conflicting stories printed in that morning's papers.

Tony's negative test results in her feature had offset the demand Jack had made in his piece for more drug testing. Her feature had been picked up in some of the biggest cities in the United States. She'd saved Tony's career and made her own.

A voice over the intercom announced the Rays' flight would leave in fifteen minutes. Weather delays had grounded their flight for several hours past their scheduled departure. Amanda was more than a little glad she was taking a later flight.

She worked her way through the crowd toward Reggie. She found him chatting with Brad. Under other circumstances she would worry about these two coming in contact. Today she was riding a career high and couldn't be bothered. Let people find out about her and Brad.

Brad's gaze touched hers as she approached. In his favorite faded jeans and a Rays' shirt and Windbreaker, he looked good-ol'-boy yummy and she couldn't wait to get him alone and strip him naked.

Eager to whisper her naughty thoughts in his ear, Amanda quickened her steps, only to be cut off by Jack. "I guess we both won this one."

"How's that, Jack?"

"Fox News called. They want us both on their show. The two competitors battling for victory."

"I'm not interested," she said. It was true. She didn't want to fight him. She wanted the job at *L.A. Woman.* "You can have the glory all by yourself."

He arched his eyebrow. "I see. You want the spotlight all by your lonesome or not at all." He shrugged. "You'll never beat me, Amanda. You might keep up, but you'll never take the lead."

"I don't want the lead. You win." She started walking, focused on reaching Brad's side.

"Amanda!"

She looked right to see Tony approach. He held out his hand and she shook it.

"Thank you," he said. "What you did saved my ass."

Amanda grinned. "This didn't exactly work out badly for me, you know."

"Hey, Amanda." Casey joined them.

Though the rookie still got on her nerves, after interviewing him she'd decided he wasn't all that bad. He talked big but she suspected that covered insecurities, rather than representing true arrogance.

"My agent got a call from *Sports Illustrated,*" he said. "They read your feature and took interest. Looks like I might just make the cover."

"That's huge," Amanda said, excited for him. "Congratulations."

"Yeah, man," Tony added, patting the kid's back. "We've had our words, but you have talent. Good things come when it's time."

"You think I have talent?"

"Of course, I do. We all do, kid. But you gotta give respect where it's earned."

"I deserve respect, too," Casey said. "You guys act like Brad is the only pitcher on this team."

Amanda and Tony both answered at the same time. "That's not true."

Casey made another smart remark and Amanda decided she'd had enough. "I need to go." She turned to walk away.

"Damn, she's hot," Casey said. "I'd want her even if I hadn't bet Rogers I'd get her first."

Amanda stopped dead in her tracks, her gut balling into a tight knot. She rotated on her heels and faced him. "What?"

Tony touched her arm. "It's not what you think."

Amanda ignored Tony, focusing on Casey. "Did you make a bet with Brad over me?"

"No. Of course not."

His expression said he was lying. She felt as though she would be sick. Brad used her to win a bet? "You did," she said. "I heard you. You said you bet Brad who could get with me first." She didn't wait for an answer as she searched for Brad.

A knife had been jabbed through her heart. She'd fallen in love with a man who saw her as a prize to get before his buddies. What kind of fool did that make her?

She spotted Brad and forced her anger to the surface to keep from crying. He walked toward her and she made tracks in the opposite direction. She needed air.

She needed out of this airport and out of Brad's life. But his long legs made her escape impossible. She'd barely cleared the crowd when he caught her hand.

She whirled around. "The game is over, Brad. I know about you and Casey making that bet to get in my pants. Congratulations. You won." A single tear slid down her cheek and she swiped at it, frustrated she'd allowed him to see how he'd hurt her. "Go away."

"Oh, baby." He pulled her close despite her efforts to evade his hold. "I already told you I can't do that."

"I'm not some groupie you can play games with. Let go of me."

"Betting the kid was stupid, Amanda, and it meant nothing."

"Are you crazy? People are watching us."

"Let them watch because I'm not going anywhere until I say what I have to say." He pressed his cheek to hers, lips near her ear and held her close. "Reach in my right pocket."

"Brad—"

"Please. Just do it. Hear me out. Then if you want me to go, I will. I'll leave and never bother you again."

Her heart thudded and the feel of his body pressed to hers lulled her under a spell. She hesitated, then reached into his pocket. Her fingers curled around a small velvet box.

A ring box.

She pulled it out and Brad leaned back enough to look at her. "Open it."

She flipped the lid up and a giant diamond stared back at her. "What...what is this?"

"I love you, Amanda." He reached inside the box for the ring. "You're the one. I know we haven't known each other long but it's long enough for me to know I want to spend the rest of my life with you. Marry me. Elope with me tonight or wear that ring for two years. However long it takes for you to be as sure as I am."

Her head spun with his words. Tears of happiness filled her eyes. Brad loved her. "I love you, too, Brad."

He took her left hand in his. "Enough to wear my ring?"

"Yes," she whispered, barely able to find her voice for the emotion welling up inside her.

Brad slid the ring on her finger and cheering filled the air. They faced the press, cameras flashing all around them. Brad glanced at her, mischief flashing in those deep-blue eyes a second before he reached down and picked her up.

Amanda gasped, her arms going around his neck. "What are you doing?"

"Taking you home with me. Where you belong."

"You just made a lot of reporters very happy. We're going to be all over the papers."

He nuzzled her neck. "As long as I make this reporter happy, that's all that matters."

Epilogue

Six months later

THE EVENING before Amanda's wedding, her parents hosted dinner. Brad's mom attended, as did Kelli. After dessert, the women had gathered over last-minute wedding preparations and girl talk. The men did what they loved. They worshipped the Mustangs in the garage.

Ready to bring the night to a close, Amanda found her father standing in front of '67 Mustang coupe. Brad was underneath, only his feet and legs showing. Her father smiled. "How's the bride?"

She gave him a big hug. "Nervous, Daddy." She winked to let her father know she was up to no good. "I'm really, really nervous."

He lowered his voice to a loud whisper as if he was being discreet. "You're not having cold feet, are you?"

"I guess I am," she said, her voice full of exaggerated worry. "I think this was a mistake."

Brad rolled out from underneath the car, his face pale. "What did you say?"

Amanda and her father started laughing. "I said, get your butt up here and kiss me goodbye. I'm going to Kelli's for the night."

He grabbed a towel and wiped his hands before

pushing to his feet. He put his arms around her and kissed her forehead. "Don't scare me like that. And I still don't know why we can't be together tonight."

"Because we can't," she said, "and I'm not going to try to explain again because you don't want to hear it, anyway. And I am nervous. Half the world is coming to our wedding." Despite their desire to keep things small, the event had snowballed into a massive social gathering. Brad had re-signed with the Rays, so his team would be attending. On top of the Rays, many of her father's team members were also coming.

The *L.A. Woman* editors had convinced Amanda and Brad to allow them to do a special feature on the wedding now that she was their employee. Reggie would be the photographer. She'd appreciated his work enough to ask him along for the ride. Apparently, that was how Jack had burned him. Jack had promised Reggie a future he hadn't delivered.

Amanda thought of all those eyes on her path down the aisle. "I can just see me tripping in the ridiculously high-heeled shoes Kelli talked me into buying and embarrassing us both."

"Telephone, Daddy," Kelli said, appearing in the doorway. "One of the players."

He sighed. "I never get a night off."

"And you love it," Kelli and Amanda said at the same time.

Kelli snapped her fingers at Amanda. "Come on, woman. You need your beauty sleep." She eyed Brad. "And you might want to make sure that best man of yours gets plenty of sleep, too."

Brad arched his eyebrow. "I don't think Kurt is worried about his beauty sleep."

"But he will need his energy. I'm a rather demanding maid of honor."

"Behave, Kelli. This is my wedding."

"Since when do weddings demand good behavior?"

Bill poked his head in the room. "Your pager just went off."

"Oh, good grief," Kelli protested. "Now, I can't get a day off." She narrowed her gaze on Amanda. "Do your whole kiss-kiss, bye-bye thing and come on."

Brad waved her off. "Go answer your page. She'll be there in a minute."

"She better be," Kelli said, talking as she exited. "I'm serious about her beauty sleep."

"I'm beginning to think we should have eloped," Amanda said.

"We still could," he suggested, his eyes lighting with the idea.

"Hmm," she murmured, as his lips brushed hers, teasing her with their soft touch. "Tempting, but a lot of people would be upset if we didn't show up for our own wedding."

He smiled at her, tenderness in his eyes. "I guess I can share you with them tomorrow. As long as I get forever." His fingers trailed down her cheek. "I love you, Amanda."

"I love you, too, Brad."

And for the first time in Amanda's life, she believed in happily ever after. Oh, she knew they'd have fights. But somehow, Brad always made her laugh when she thought she was too mad to do anything but scream. And he made her feel safe and confident. He had become more than her lover. Brad had become her best friend.

* * * * *

Welcome to cowboy country...

Turn the page for a sneak preview of
TEXAS BABY
by
Kathleen O'Brien
An exciting new title from Harlequin Superromance
for everyone who loves stories about the West.

Harlequin Superromance—
Where life and love weave together in
emotional and unforgettable ways.

CHAPTER ONE

CHASE TRANSFERRED his gaze to the road and identified a foreign spot on the horizon. A car. Almost half a mile away, where the straight, tree-lined drive met the public road. He could tell it was coming too fast, but judging the speed of a vehicle moving straight toward you was tricky.

It wasn't until it was about two hundred yards away that he realized the driver must be drunk...or crazy. Or both.

The guy was going maybe sixty. On a private drive, out here in ranch country, where kids or horses or tractors or stupid chickens might come darting out any minute, that was criminal. Chase straightened from his comfortable slouch and waved his hands.

"Slow down, you fool," he called out. He took the porch steps quickly and began walking fast down the driveway.

The car veered oddly, from one lane to another, then up onto the slight rise of the thick green spring grass. It just barely missed the fence.

"Slow down, damn it!"

He couldn't see the driver, and he didn't recognize this automobile. It was small and old, and couldn't have cost much even when it was new. It was probably white, but now it needed either a wash or a new paint job or both.

"Damn it, what's wrong with you?"

At the last minute, he had to jump away, because the idiot behind the wheel clearly wasn't going to turn to avoid a collision. He couldn't believe it. The car kept coming, finally slowing a little, but it was too late.

Still going about thirty miles an hour, it slammed into the large, white-brick pillar that marked the front boundaries of the house. The pillar wasn't going to give an inch, so the car had to. The front end folded up like a paper fan.

It seemed to take forever for the car to settle, as if the trauma happened in slow motion, reverberating from the front to the back of the car in ripples of destruction. The front windshield suddenly seemed to ice over with lethal bits of glassy frost. Then the side windows exploded.

The front driver's door wrenched open, as if the car wanted to expel its contents. Metal buckled hideously. Small pieces, like hubcaps and mirrors, skipped and ricocheted insanely across the oyster-shell driveway.

Finally, everything was still. Into the silence, a plume of steam shot up like a geyser, smelling of rust and heat. Its snakelike hiss almost smothered the low, agonized moan of the driver.

Chase's anger had disappeared. He didn't feel anything but a dull sense of disbelief. Things like this didn't happen in real life. Not in his life. Maybe the sun had actually put him to sleep….

But he was already kneeling beside the car. The driver was a woman. The frosty glass-ice of the windshield was dotted with small flecks of blood. She must have hit it with her head, because just below her hairline a red liquid was seeping out. He touched it. He tried to wipe it away before it reached her eyebrow, though, of course, that made no sense at all. Her eyes were shut.

Was she conscious? Did he dare move her? Her dress was covered in glass, and the metal of the car was sticking out lethally in all the wrong places.

Then he remembered, with an intense relief, that every good medical man in the county was here, just behind the house, drinking his champagne. He found his phone and paged Trent.

The woman moaned.

Alive, then. Thank God for that.

He saw Trent coming toward him, starting out at a lope, but quickly switching to a full run.

"Get Dr. Marchant," Chase called. "Don't bother with 911."

Trent didn't take long to assess the situation. A fraction of a second, and he began pulling out his cell phone and running toward the house.

The yelling seemed to have roused the woman. She opened her eyes. They were blue and clouded with pain and confusion.

"Chase," she said.

His breath stalled. His head pulled back. "What?"

Her only answer was another moan, and he wondered if he had imagined the word. He reached around her and put his arm behind her shoulders. She was tiny. Probably petite by nature, but surely way too thin. He could feel her shoulder blades pushing against her skin, as fragile as the wishbone in a turkey.

She seemed to have passed out, so he put his other arm under her knees and lifted her out. He tried to avoid the jagged metal, but her skirt caught on a piece and the tearing sound seemed to wake her again.

"No," she said. "Please."

"I'm just trying to help," he said. "It's going to be all right."

She seemed profoundly distressed. She wriggled in his arms, and she was so weak, like a broken bird. It made him feel too big and brutish. And intrusive. As if touching her this way, his bare hands against the warm skin behind her knees, were somehow a transgression.

He wished he could be more delicate. But he smelled gasoline, and he knew it wasn't safe to leave her here.

Finally he heard the sound of voices, as guests began to run around the side of the house, alerted by Trent. Dr. Marchant was at the front, racing toward them as if he were forty instead of seventy. Susannah was right behind him, her green dress floating around her trim legs.

"Please," the woman in his arms murmured again. She looked at him, the expression in her blue eyes lost and bewildered. He wondered if she might be on drugs. Hitting her head on the windshield might account for this unfocused, glazed look, but it couldn't explain the crazy driving.

"Please, put me down. Susannah… The wedding…"

Chase's arms tightened instinctively, and he froze in his tracks. She whimpered, and he realized he might be hurting her. "Say that again?"

"The wedding. I have to stop it."

* * * * *

Be sure to look for TEXAS BABY,
available September 11, 2007,
as well as other fantastic Superromance titles
available in September.

When four bold, risk-taking women
challenge themselves and
each other...no man is safe!

Harlequin Blaze brings you

THE MARTINI DARES

A brand-new sexy miniseries from
award-winning authors

Lori Wilde

Carrie Alexander

Isabel Sharpe

Jamie Denton

DON'T MISS BOOK 1,

MY SECRET LIFE
by Lori Wilde

Available September 2007
wherever books are sold.

HARLEQUIN®

Mediterranean NIGHTS™

Experience glamour, elegance, mystery and revenge aboard the high seas....

Coming in September 2007...

BREAKING ALL THE RULES

by

Marisa Carroll

Aboard the cruise ship *Alexandra's Dream* for some R & R, sports journalist Lola Sandler is surprised to spot pro-golfer Eric Lashman. Years after walking away from the pro circuit with no explanation to the public, Eric now finds himself teaching aboard a cruise ship.

Lola smells a career-making exposé... but their developing relationship may force her to make a difficult choice.

REQUEST YOUR FREE BOOKS!

2 FREE NOVELS PLUS 2 FREE GIFTS!

HARLEQUIN®

Blaze.

Red-hot reads!

YES! Please send me 2 FREE Harlequin® Blaze® novels and my 2 FREE gifts. After receiving them, if I don't wish to receive any more books, I can return the shipping statement marked "cancel." If I don't cancel, I will receive 6 brand-new novels every month and be billed just $3.99 per book in the U.S., or $4.47 per book in Canada, plus 25¢ shipping and handling per book and applicable taxes, if any*. That's a savings of at least 15% off the cover price! I understand that accepting the 2 free books and gifts places me under no obligation to buy anything. I can always return a shipment and cancel at any time. Even if I never buy another book from Harlequin, the two free books and gifts are mine to keep forever.

151 HDN EF3W   351 HDN EF3X

Name	(PLEASE PRINT)	
Address		Apt.
City	State/Prov.	Zip/Postal Code

Signature (if under 18, a parent or guardian must sign)

Mail to the **Harlequin Reader Service®**:
IN U.S.A.: P.O. Box 1867, Buffalo, NY 14240-1867
IN CANADA: P.O. Box 609, Fort Erie, Ontario L2A 5X3

Not valid to current Harlequin Blaze subscribers.

Want to try two free books from another line?
Call 1-800-873-8635 or visit www.morefreebooks.com.

* Terms and prices subject to change without notice. NY residents add applicable sales tax. Canadian residents will be charged applicable provincial taxes and GST. This offer is limited to one order per household. All orders subject to approval. Credit or debit balances in a customer's account(s) may be offset by any other outstanding balance owed by or to the customer. Please allow 4 to 6 weeks for delivery.

Your Privacy: Harlequin is committed to protecting your privacy. Our Privacy Policy is available online at www.eHarlequin.com or upon request from the Reader Service. From time to time we make our lists of customers available to reputable firms who may have a product or service of interest to you. If you would prefer we not share your name and address, please check here.

HB07

ATHENA FORCE

Heart-pounding romance and thrilling adventure.

Professional negotiator Lindsey Novak is faced with her biggest challenge—to buy back Teal Arnett, a young woman with unique powers. In the process Lindsey uncovers a devastating plot that involves scientists from around the globe, and all of them lead to one woman who is bent on destroying Athena Academy...at any cost.

LOOK FOR

THE GOOD THIEF
by Judith Leon

Available September wherever you buy books.

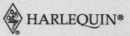

HARLEQUIN®

Blaze™

COMING NEXT MONTH

#345 KIDNAPPED! Jo Leigh
Forbidden Fantasies

She had a secret desire to be kidnapped and held against her will.... But when heiress Tate Baxter's fantasy game turns out to be all too real, can sexy bodyguard Michael Caulfield put aside his feelings and rescue her in time?

#346 MY SECRET LIFE Lori Wilde
The Martini Dares, Bk. 1

Kate Winfield's secrets were safe until hottie Liam James came along. Now the sexy bachelor with the broad chest and winning smile is insisting he wants to uncover the delectable Katie—from head to toe.

#347 OVEREXPOSED Leslie Kelly
The Bad Girls Club, Bk. 3

Isabella Natale works in the family bakery by day, but at night her velvet mask and G-string drive men wild. Her double life is a secret, even from Nick Santori, the club's hot new bodyguard who's always treated her like a kid. Now she's planning to show the man of her dreams that while it's okay to look, it's *much* better to touch....

#348 SWEPT AWAY Dawn Atkins
Sex on the Beach

Her plan was simple. Candy Calder would use her vacation to show her boss Matt Rockwell she was serious about her job. But her plan backfired when he invited her to enjoy the sinful side of Malibu. With an offer this tempting, what girl could refuse?

#349 SHIVER AND SPICE Kelley St. John
The Sexth Sense, Bk. 3

She's not alive. She's not dead. She's something in between. And medium Dax Vicknair wants her desperately! Dax fell madly in love with teacher Celeste Beauchamp when he helped one of her students cross over. He thought he was destined to live without her. But now Celeste is back—and Dax intends to make the most of their borrowed time....

#350 THE NAKED TRUTH Shannon Hollis
Million Dollar Secrets, Bk. 3

Risk taker Eve Best is on the verge of having everything she's ever wanted. But what she really wants is the handsome buttoned-down executive Mitchell Hayes, who must convince the gorgeous talk-show host to say "yes" to his business offer *and* his very private proposition....

www.eHarlequin.com

HBCNM0807